Valdessia

Dawn of the Aborrent

Charles McGinniss

The Curious Duo, LLC

Concept, Story, World and Characters created by: Charles McGinniss

BookCover by: **Cande Carballo**

Ghostwritten by: Phil-Domo

Edited by: Rosemary Lawton

ISBN: 979-8-9989943-0-2(ebook)

ISBN: 979-8-9989943-1-9 (PaperBack)

ISBN: 979-8-9989943-2-6 (Hardcover)

First edition 2025

Visit our site for more information and upcoming news. https://thecuriousduollc.com/valdessia

Contents

Chapter 1

It was a spectacle of violence. Weapons clashed. Blood was spilled. Flames scorched at flesh and stone shattered bones. With each additional step in the macabre dance, the crowd's cheers grew ever louder. It became so riotous that it drowned out any of the action going on below.

Tara wished they would quiet down a bit and listen. Focusing only on the Corbinite Trials' more excessive elements misses their essence. The real heart of the competition was in the shorthand spoken between members of a team as they coordinated their efforts, the chides between rivals as they tried to get into each other's heads, the precise, intricate gestures as the spellcasters brought forth the might of the Tether. Certainly, that was all more exciting than a quick flash of fire when someone accidentally triggers a pressure plate and gets to briefly experience what it is like to be inside a barbeque.

Fortunately for Tara, her spectator's box came with a handy little Magi-Tek device to enhance her experience. The scrying tablet inlaid in the center table linked to invisible sensors scattered throughout the contest grounds, giving Tara a close-up look at the action. With a flick of her finger across the tablet, she could swap between sensors, giving her various camera angles of the action. While she could do without seeing every bead of sweat and drop of blood, the important thing was that the sound also emanated from the tablet, allowing her to hear the important bits over the roar of the crowd.

"They're coming into the last stretch now." Marzin leaned over the railing, preferring to watch the action below with his own eyes instead of through the tablet. "The Rainecourt team is trailing, but the finale is where things get interesting. Theres plenty of time to catch up."

Alarus, seated beside Tara, seemed disinterested in the competition. Giving Marzin a disapproving look. "You should at least pretend to take your position seriously, Commander. How would the king react if he knew the man tasked with protecting his daughter was allowing himself to become so captivated in the game when he should be on duty?"

Marzin chuckled. "His highness would be too engrossed himself to notice. You should have seen how disappointed he was when he realized he couldn't make it."

The crowd roared as a competitor from Team Lymeria triggered a blasting trap on the first step of the center platform. He had been getting reckless—but didn't really have many other choices, being the last standing member of his team. Really, it was impressive that he had made it as far as he did by himself. As the smoke cleared, all that remained was a faint purple glow lingering in the air just above a smattering of blood on the platform, evidence of the work of the Nexus bracelet the competitor was wearing.

Despite the crowd's enthusiasm for blood spilling, very few competitors actually died, thanks to those bracelets. They took advantage of the unique Tether found here on the unique island of Nexus that allowed manipulation of time and space. As Tara understood, this was because of the dual glyphs placed upon the bracelets: one dedicated to looking a second into the competitor's future, and the other acted to transport them to the infirmary a moment before their deaths. With the healers present, most would be back to perfect health within the hour. Unless your death was nearly instantaneous, your risk of dying during the trial was actually pretty low—however grisly the spectacle might appear from the stands. All the pain, however, was entirely too real.

"Only two teams remaining!" Marzin exclaimed with excitement. Lymerians were again favored. Now only the Elondor team stands between us and bringing the crown back to Rainecourt!"

Tara was amused by this aspect of the commander. He was an older man, with his hair mid-transition between blond and silver, giving him a distinguished look—one that was further enhanced by his immaculate grooming and perfectly pressed uniform. His attitude usually matched his appearance, as he took his duties as the leader of the royal guard seriously, but today he was acting like a boy who had just been let loose in a toy store.

"You participated in the trials once yourself, didn't you, Commander?" Tara asked.

Marzin nodded. "A lifetime ago, but yes, princess. Ah, it all brings back memories. The roar of the crowds, the faint ozone smell from the Tether in the air, the feelings of excitement and fear and adrenaline. Representing Rainecourt here on Nexus, in the trials, still ranks as one of my proudest moments as a swordmaster."

Alarus scoffed. "Correct me if my history is spotty, but Rainecourt came in second that year, did it not?"

The Commander narrowed his eyes towards the High Mage for a moment, before he sighed and looked back towards the contest below. "Aye. Victory eluded us at the end. Hopefully, our team this year does not repeat our mistakes."

Through the tablet, Tara watched as both remaining teams neared the center of the contest grounds. Having collected enough flags, the winner would simply be the first to reach the end. Team Elondori reached the center first and ascended the central platform. Despite the many traps, the platform provided a safer, shorter route, bypassing a challenging obstacle as a Lymerian competitor unfortunately discovered.

When Team Rainecourt reached the center, they were left with no choice but to take the shorter, but more dangerous, lower path across the field if they hoped to gain any ground on the leaders. Teams avoided the lower path; they soon discovered why.

The ground opened up to reveal a massive cage. The beast inside was ten feet tall, stood on four legs in a manner similar to a wolf, and was covered in dark red scales. It opened its massive jaw and a plume of smoke drifted out.

"What is that?" Tara asked. It was unlike any creature she had come across in her studies.

Alarus scratched at his unkempt beard. "Pryosenius Senti, colloquially called a pyrosaur. A predator from the Plane of Fire, and one of the very few creatures that likes to munch on daemons. Which probably gives you an idea of how dangerous they are. Mistress Gea's conjurers really outdid themselves this year. Hopefully, they're able to keep control of it after it has finished making a meal out of our team."

"Hey, don't count our team out yet!" Marzin argued. "They can take that beastie down."

The High Mage waved a hand dismissively. "Perhaps. If the melee fighters can control their egos and give the mages the space to do their work."

The Commander did not rise to the mage's bait. They bickered incessantly. Alarus was a stark contrast to the serious and composed swordmaster. He was a grouchy old man. Short and wiry due to his Kray ancestry, you might mistake him at first glance for a vagrant given his greasy white hair, scruffy beard, and the wrinkled, stained dress that seemed to be the only outfit in his wardrobe. But there was no one in the kingdom with a better grasp on applied magics, and Tara was glad he accepted her invitation to accompany her in observing the trials. She had learned much from his insights into the competitors' glyphs and foci.

Down in the contest grounds, the cage surrounding the beast dropped, leaving the four competitors of Team Rainecourt to contend with it if they wished to progress. The team's swordfighter, a young man with golden hair and a cocky smirk, was already rushing forward before the cage had even settled.

"I'll keep its attention on me!" he shouted, his voice clear through the tablet. "Hit it hard while it's distracted!"

The swordfighter ducked under a swipe from the creature's massive claws and struck up in return. His sword clashed against the beast's underarm but seemed to barely leave a scratch on its thick hide. The pyrosaur roared and spun around to hit the competitor with its tail, which the swordfighter was able to leap over. He landed gracefully on one foot and spun as if to ready to make another strike, only to find the creature arching its head back, flames spewing from its mouth.

"Shit," the swordfighter exclaimed as he realized he did not have the time or space to avoid the coming spew of fire.

The pyrosaur lurched forward and brought forth a tremendous wave of flames. Tara could feel the heat all the way from her box far above the action.

Before the wave of flame could engulf the swordfighter, the team's shield bearer rushed in front of him. The glyphs on his shield flared to life as he held it against the oppressive wave of scorching flame. The shield bearer strained as if pushed back against an immense weight.

"Any time now!" he growled.

As if on cue, the roar of flames suddenly was exchanged with a strangled cry as what appeared to be silvery wire wrapped tightly around its neck. Similar wires appeared around its front legs and began to pull them forward, forcing the beast to bend toward the ground.

The wires connected to the many rings worn on the fingers of the team's utility mage, serving as her foci. Her hands moved in broad circles as bright glyphs formed around her. Tara knew the glyphs were specific to the spell and required a great amount of concentration, paired with the arcane gestures of their hands, and allowed mages to dictate the form the Tether would take after it was enhanced through their focus. She admired how they were able to maintain their concentration in the field, especially in combat. Alarus said that the mages had a connection to their specific plane from which the Tether flowed and that the foci amplified the casting of spells from that plane. There were a variety of different planes and it was always fascinating to see what the mages could conjure.

The beast roared in defiance, trying to pull itself free as the wires continued to tighten and drag it towards the ground.

It struck out suddenly with its hind legs, surprising Tara—and the competitors—with its ability to snap its rear legs forward at such an extreme angle that it could hit in front of its body. Despite retreating, the mage was still sent flying by the chest impact. She was not transported away, though, so that force must not have been enough to threaten her life. It did cost her the concentration on her Tether, and the creature let out a triumphant roar as it tore free from its constraints.

The team's final member was already in action. The war mage's hand was filled with tiny, glowing seeds. He dashed between the creature's legs while arcane glyphs formed around him.

He threw the seeds at the pyrosaur's face, and they quickly grew into large, thorny vines that wrapped themselves around the creature's eyes, blinding him. She could only imagine how the creature was faring with those things erupting and enclosing its eyes, effectively blindfolding it.

Sure enough, the creature cried out in distress and shook its head wildly as it was blinded by the thick, thorny vines. The crowd cheered wildly. Anything that flashy was always a crowd pleaser.

The creature spewed another plume of fire, but it could no longer see where the competitors were and they were able to stay well clear of its path. The shield bearer helped the utility mage to her feet, and the team seemed ready to progress.

"While it's hindered, let's get past," the shield bearer declared.

"Oh, come on," the swordfighter said. "That's not what the crowd came here for. They want to see us bring that thing down!"

Not waiting to listen to the arguments of his teammates, the swordfighter rushed at the creature once more. He was easily able to dodge the blinded beast's wild swipes, get around its side, and jump up onto its tail. While the crowd cheered him on, he climbed its back until he reached the beast's head, brought his sword up high, and plunged it deep into one of the creature's eyes. He buried the sword to its hilt.

The pyrosaur let out a pained cry that almost had Tara feeling pity for it even though Tara knew that all the beasts in the Mistress's challenges had glyphs incorporated onto them to save them from death as well as protect her investment. The creature wobbled unsteadily on its feet as its life bled out through this grievous wound.

But it was not going to go out without one last burst of fury. It swiped at its face with its claws, smacking the swordfighter off of it. He landed with a thud on the ground below, groaning from the impact. With one last roar, the beast let out a final bellow of flame, this one brighter and more intense than any that came before it. The swordfighter could not get away, nor could any of his allies get to his aid in time. He was engulfed, and by the time the flames faded, only the purple haze of the Nexus bracelet's transportation magic remained.

The beast also disappeared in a purple haze just before succumbing once and for all to its injury.

"I knew something like this would happen," the war mage sighed.

"Honestly surprised it took this long," the utility mage agreed.

The shield bearer gestured forward. "Contest's not over. We can still do this. Let's go!"

Tara's fixation on the competition was broken when the door to her spectator's box was opened. Captain Denbar, the last of Tara's guests, had finally returned. Just in time for the contest's climax.

"Apologies for my absence, princess," he said with a slight bow.

"That was a long time on the shitter," Alarus remarked. "Everything all right?"

Denbar put a hand to his stomach. "It's just the food here. Always gives me problems."

The mage exchanged a look with Tara, and she knew what he was thinking. Denbar had earned an impressive number of commendations during his service with the Rainecourt Navy, enough to earn himself an invite to join the princess in spectating the trials. But it was something of an open secret that he struggled with a gambling addiction. More than once he'd come to the royal family, hat in hand, asking for help with his debtors.

The captain had reptilian eyes, a sign of his lyrian ancestry, which could make him a little hard to read, but Tara had been around him enough to tell when he was nervous.

Whatever bet he had been making on the outcome of these games, it must have been a big one. Hopefully it was at least on the home team.

"Well, you're back just in time, captain," Tara said. "We're down to the final two teams. Rainecourt's still in the running, though we are down a man and trailing a bit behind."

Denbar nodded and returned to his seat just as the crowd began to pick up its raucousness once more. Tara turned back to the tablet to see what had gotten them so excited.

She nearly let out a cheer herself. The Rainecourt team had made up the distance and had arrived at the far side of the grounds just as the other team had descended the platform. The two teams were now neck and neck, with nothing between them and the finish line.

Nothing besides each other.

A water mage on the Elondori team acted first. With well-practiced arm gestures, a bright and large glyph was forming in front of her. She completed the glyph by clasping her hands together, and the necklace which served as her focus started to glow.

Water burst forth from the ground in front of her. The water spewing from the fountain coalesced, formed an impressive wave, and came crashing down on the opposing team. It wasn't going to be enough to do much more than slow the team down, though, so Tara wondered what the strategy was.

Her question was quickly answered by the Elondori swordfighter as he followed behind the wave, matching its base as it slid its way towards the Rainecourt team. It was a masking maneuver, Tara realized, allowing the swordfighter to close in on the opposing team without being spotted. Very clever. It was seeing these kinds of unique applications of Tether that made these games so exciting.

The Rainecourt team stood their ground against the wave, and though they were a little drenched, they were no worse for the wear. But the gambit to conceal the Elondori swordfighter paid off, and he was within inches of the war mage before he was spotted. The war mage took a nasty cut across his side as he tried and failed to dodge out of the way of the first slash of the sword.

The shield bearer for the Rainecourt team blocked a second swing that would have taken the mage through the chest. The shield bearer and swordfighter began a melee, with the shield bearer impressively swapping between using the sharp edge of his shield as an offensive weapon and using the shield to block blows with barely a moment between the two.

Rainecourt's utility mage, meanwhile, was busy trying to engage both of Elondor's mages. She extended the silvery wires from her fingers and attempted to constrain them, but the Elondori water was maintaining a misty veil between them that obscured her vision. Meanwhile, the other mage was levitating large chunks of the stonework from the ground itself and sending it flying in her direction. The stones were chucked with little accuracy, and the utility mage was quick on her feet, but with how big they were, it seemed like only a matter of time before one of them got her.

Fortunately for team Rainecourt, their war mage wasn't quite done. While the opposing mages were distracted, he used his connection to the Plane of Nature to conjure a huge vine from beneath her, knocking her down and entangling her, causing her to lose control of her mists. With the veil gone, the utility mage seized the opportunity and quickly wrapped the other Elondori mage in her conjured wires.

Meanwhile, the melee turned to the favor of the shield bearer, whose outstanding skill allowed him to overcome the swordfighter despite only having his shield as a weapon. With a final *slam* into the side of the swordfighter's head, the shield bearer emerged victorious. Everything seemed to turn out in the favor of the Rainecourt team. Victory was within their grasp.

But just then, a bell was sounded. A victor had been declared. Team Elondor was the winner of this year's Corbinite Trials.

It took a moment to realize what had happened. Team Elondor still had all four of its members, while Rainecourt had been reduced to three. While three members stayed behind to fight, the fourth had slipped away to make a break for the finish. While Team Rainecourt had won the combat, they had lost the game.

Tara felt a wave of great disappointment, and she was not alone. There were several jeers from the audience. Everyone wanted a climactic finish, and seeing one team win through deception wasn't satisfying. Still, they had followed the rules and emerged as victors. They would bring back the crown to Elondor. Hopefully, this would be a lesson for the coaches of the Rainecourt team.

"I can't believe it!" Marzin yelled. He seemed to take it hardest of all. "Those sneaky Elondori snakes!"

"It isn't their fault," Alarus responded. "Our team was too full of meatheads with combat brains. Between that young swordsman who got himself killed showing off to the rest of the team so focused on the fight they didn't even realize they were missing an opponent. They were so focused on showing off their skills, they didn't consider their tactics. Kind of reminds me of someone, to be honest."

Marzin glared at him. "Oh? And who might that be?"

Alarus just smiled back at him. "Nobody important. Don't you worry."

"Our team performed their best and should be rewarded for their efforts," Tara declared, breaking up the argument. "Second place is still an impressive finish, and our competitors put on a valiant display of our nation's skills in combat and magics. Don't you agree, captain?"

Denbar didn't respond. He seemed to be just staring into space.

"Captain?" Tara repeated.

"Huh?" Debar snapped to attention. "Sorry, princess. I was lost in thought. Yes, I agree our team performed admirably. I'm sure your father will be ecstatic when he hears about how they represented the kingdom."

He must have lost a lot on whatever bets he placed, Tara thought. Otherwise, he would be practically jumping for joy right now. Maybe he bet on the home team after all. Hopefully Tara's family would not need to pay off a debt here in Nexus for him, yet again.

Marzin collected himself and put back on his serious face. "Your father wanted you to return immediately after the games were completed. We should congratulate the team on their performance and then make our way to the air docks."

Tara pouted. "There are so many interesting teams and competitors here! And maybe if we stick around, we could meet Mistress Justiciar Gea. I'd love to ask her about the time and space monolith here on Nexus. Maybe see if she will instruct me on how those bracelets work. Think of what we could do if we understood those levels of glyphs."

"Sorry, lass, but the Mistress doesn't make public appearances during the games," Alarus replied. "Well, if she does, it isn't good news for you, as she only pops her head out to deal with troublemakers."

"Besides," Marzin added, "your father was quite clear with his instructions. There have been some concerns lately in the kingdom, and you were only given permission to attend if you promised to return immediately after. If he learns that we lingered here... well, likely it would be me who got in trouble. So for my sake, I would appreciate if we followed his command."

"That's not fair, making me all concerned for you," Tara said with a sigh. "We'll also miss the closing ceremony and after party. Oh, fine. But I'm going to complain about the missed opportunity all the way home."

"Fair enough."

With that, the royal party gathered together and made their way out of the VIP spectator area down to the contest grounds. The various teams were gathering in their respective starting areas for debriefing from their coaches and to receive their accolades from the nations that they represented. Team Rainecourt had already gathered. The swordfighter who had been eliminated by the pyrosaur was among them. Tara was glad that the injuries he had received had been treated so quickly.

Marzin approached at the head of the group. "Gentlemen, congratulations on your performance today. You have done your kingdom proud. I am Commander of the Royal Guard Gavlin Marzin, and with me are Court High Mage Alarus and Royal Navy Captain Hannis Denbar. And presenting to you, Her Highness, Princess Tara Rainecourt."

The competitors bowed in respect to Tara. She always hated this part. They were the ones who had just done all the hard work while she did nothing but watch. If anything, she should be showing deference to them. But Marzin was a stickler for royal protocols.

"You all put on an exciting performance," Tara declared. "I was at the edge of my seat the entire time. You should all be very proud of what you accomplished today."

Most of them nodded respectfully, but the young swordfighter looked away in shame.

"I am sorry, princess," he said. "I cost us the crown. If I had acted more responsibly, followed the will of my teammates, we wouldn't have been a man down at the end and would have won."

Tara smiled at him. "I actually found it really exciting, watching you take down the pyrosaur. Tell me, how did you know its eye was its weak point?"

The swordfighter looked surprised. "Oh, uh... during our practices, we had quite a few drills on how to combat planar creatures. One of the tricks we were taught is that, though many lack external sensory organs, when they do have one, it is often more vulnerable than their hide."

"Did you know that climbing up its back was going to be the best way to get access to his head, or were there other methods in your mind if the battle had unfolded differently?" Tara asked. "Also, I believe your sword style blends three different styles I've seen before. Is that a combination of your own innovation or is there a swordmaster out there who trains in those styles specifically? Was your sword picked out more for planar creature encounters or for combat against the other teams' swordsmen? What would you say is your best tactic for getting within melee range of a mage who has already begun casting?" Tara could hardly contain her enthusiasm to learn new tactics. Although out of breath, she stood in eager anticipation of his reply.

The swordfighter was absolutely flabbergasted now. "I... well... uhm..."

Marvin pushed Tara aside. "I apologize. The princess is very *excited* about your performance. All of you. If I let her, she would be asking you to break down your battle tactics second by second. As I've said, you have our congratulations, and an assurance that when you return to Rainecourt, it will be with all the honor you deserve. Now if you'll excuse us, we have an airship to catch."

Tara groaned at being cut off without getting her answers, but she knew it was no use. She curtsied towards the competitors. "Thank you for representing our home so well."

They left behind a very surprised team, including a completely stunned swordfighter, as they made their way out of the contest grounds.

The Lord of the Skies was the pride of the Rainecourt Royal Navy. It was one of the largest airships in the world, the result of a pact with the kray of The Emberstone Syndicate. This was a new design of airships. The ship was built encasing the main ballonet. This provided much better protection to the air container. The front of the ship surrounding the ballonet resembled the front of a large galleon. The back part around the ballonet was a corbinite alloy that was not as impenetrable as pure corbinite, but it was much lighter. At the top of the ship was the engine, with two large smokestacks. The steam engines were an advanced prototype that the kray had yet to put in another ship, one that made the *Lord* faster and more maneuverable than other ships in its size class. Magi-tek, a merging of magic with engineering, was used to power the steam engine. Fire and water glyphs were engraved on the steam engine to produce the steam, and had to be recharged regularly to keep the ship operating at full capacity. The steam engine was used to power two huge, encased propellers on the sides of the ship. There wasn't another ship in the kingdom that could both handle the harsh skies that surrounded the isle of Nexus and could make the trip between Nexus and Aurelia's Hold, the capital of Rainecourt, in a couple of days.

Normally, being on the ship filled Tara with a combination of pride and wonder. She had insisted on being on its maiden flight even when her father had been concerned about the untested nature of the engine. But now its speed reminded her that she will be returning home faster than she would wish. Once she got back, her moment of excitement being far from home and watching the best in the world compete in tests of strength and skill would be over. She'd be expected to go back to the dull parts of her royal duties, under the care of her overprotective family and guards that prevented her from doing much else. Who knew when she would next get an opportunity for such an adventure?

"You seem awfully glum, princess," Alarus noted.

She gazed past him in thought. "I'm just dreading my loss of momentary freedom. You think I proved myself during this trip to make Father less concerned about me going out from the castle on my own?"

Alarus scratched at his beard. "Perhaps in better times. There have been some rumors surrounding the royal court that have your father on edge. Until things settle, give him a little slack. He's just concerned about you."

That wasn't the first time Tara had heard about these rumors, but nobody had seen fit to share any details with her. "What rumors?"

The mage seemed to contemplate sharing with her, but just when Tara thought she would finally get some solid answers, the ship suddenly jolted. That was followed by an alarm blaring, one that Tara had only ever heard before during drills. It was a combat station's alarm.

They were under attack.

"Well, that sounds like trouble," Alarus remarked. "Stay here, princess. I will go see what the issue is."

Tara got up from the table. "This is my family's ship. I should assess the situation."

"Suit yourself. But if you get yourself injured, be sure to tell the Commander that I tried to stop you."

They went out to the deck, just above the rear end of the ballonet, and immediately they spotted the attackers. A dozen ships, small but quick air drifters. The type of ship told them all they needed to know about their assailants. These tiny ships were too hard to steer and too prone to engine failure for use by the navy, and it was illegal for private citizens to own a ship fitted for combat. That only left one option.

"Pirates," Alarus voiced. "This was supposed to be a relaxing trip, too."

The *Lord* made a sudden sharp turn, causing Tara to clutch onto the railing for support, as it was trying to maneuver out of the range of the assailing vessels. But while the capital ship was fast and agile for a ship its size, it couldn't hope to outmaneuver the drifters.

Weapons fired from the prow of the ship. Massive cannons fired their explosive payloads at the drifters. These weapons were designed for combat between capital ships, though, not for taking out small assailants. In typical air battle, the *Lord* would be accompanied by several support ships and fighters to protect it from the smaller vessels. But they were flying in friendly space during peace time—no one had thought that they would need a full escort.

A single pirate ship exploded from the impact of a cannon shot. But the others were getting ever closer. The *Lord* shook as it took shot after shot from the spear-throwers at the front of the drifters.

"Do I have to do everything around here?" Alarus asked.

He raised his fingers before him in an intricate, arcane gesture, bright yellow glyphs beginning to form around his hands as his focus bracelet glowed.

Around one of the pirate ships, a hand composed of stone materialized. It was larger than the entire drifter and seemed to hold the ship in its palm. Slowly, the hand closed. There was a screech that could be heard all the way from the deck of the *Lord* as the drifter's frame began to bend and crack under the weight of this closing fist. Finally, the engine was impacted by the pressure, causing the entire ship to explode.

It was a good start, but two ships down still left ten to go. And they were out of time. The *Lord* shook again, harder this time. Tara was thrown off her feet and onto the deck.

The blaring alarm changed its pattern. It was no longer signaling for combat stations.

Now it was a warning that they had been boarded.

Chapter 2

It was the early morning, or as close to it as Amaura could reason. With the perpetual haze that hung over Bloodstone, it was impossible to truly know the time of day. Only the faintest bit of light was visible through the fog emanating from the Dusk Towers, enough to know it was no longer nighttime, but not enough to harm the light-sensitive skin of the necrids. She sometimes wondered what it would be like to awaken to the sun at dawn and retire when the sun does at dusk, as she had heard from the stories of those slaves brought in from foreign lands. It sounded more pleasant than arising whenever the bell chimed, signaling her mistress had summoned her, and only being allowed to sleep when it was deemed there were no more pressing tasks for her to do.

Well, soon that would change. Her Ascension ceremony was right around the corner, and she would be elevated from slave to necrid. It hardly seemed real, that all the hard work she had put in, the days of toil that went back to the earliest memories of her childhood, were finally about to be rewarded, and she would join the ranks of the lords. How did a necrid know when to awake without someone ordering them to, she pondered. It was a good problem to have.

But for the moment, she was still a slave and still had to complete the tasks that had been laid out for her. Last thing she wanted was to give them a reason to delay her Ascension now that she was so close. Even if the tasks she had been assigned were unsavory.

The Listeria Blood Bank was at the end of a row of processing centers. The pleasant white and black spiral work in front of the otherwise unremarkable buildings did little to mask the horrors that took place inside. Half-prison, half-extraction chambers, the processing centers treated the slaves unfortunate enough to wind up there as little more than cattle, extracting every ounce of blood from their livestock as was possible without outright killing them. While not being drained, their lives consisted of sitting in dark cages while strapped to feeding tubes. Amaura had been brought to tour those facilities as a child whenever she didn't closely obey an order, a warning from her mistress as to what fate awaited a displeasing slave. Just walking by filled her with a sense of dread and anxiety.

Fortunately, her destination today was the blood bank itself, which, while the ultimate beneficiary of the sins committed in the processing centers, at least was not filling with the wails of the desperate and the dying. Outside, it was of similar design to the processing centers, though grander and with more intricacy to the spiral design. Inside was white and sterile looking, not dissimilar to an office of medicine, but instead of doctor's coats, the employees here wore expensive suits, tailor made and as crimson as blood.

The server closest to the door approached Amaura as she entered. He had the pallid white skin of a necrid and the intense gaze of a man with little patience. Under his arm, he carried a stack of the bank's "menus."

"Is there something you need, kitten?" the server asked.

Kitten was not a term of endearment but a reminder of Amaura's lyrian ancestry. Lyrian features had been morphed through their connection to the Tether of Nature eons ago, giving them some animal-like attributes. Her family's lineage was on the feline side and, for her specifically, as a thin layer of gray fur, feline ears, eyes, claws, and a tail. It seemed to be a favorite pastime of the natives to remind her that she was different. Hopefully, once she was a necrid herself, they would take a different tone.

"I've got an order here from my mistress," Amaura replied, handing over the scroll she had been carrying.

The server unfolded the scroll and quickly scanned it. "Ah, you're one of Matriarch Delmass'. Yes, we have her order ready."

He snapped his fingers, and two of the other employees rushed into the back. They returned very shortly after with two small boxes. The server opened the boxes and inspected the quality himself before handing them over to Amaura.

"It is all here," he assured her. "But tell your mistress that our supply of oni blood is running thin, so in future orders, there may be a premium applied. To make up for it, we will increase the portion sizes of Kray blood until the shortage has been resolved."

"I'll be sure to let her know," Amaura said with a bow. "Thank you very much."

Once outside, Amaura went through the boxes herself to double check they matched the order. Doing so in front of the server could have been seen as rude, but if she returned home without the order exactly as it was placed, she would be the one who was punished. She counted the vials of human, lyrian, kray, and oni blood, each marked with the region of origin and "vintage" of its source. She saw one with a disturbingly low number printed on it and tried not to imagine the child it had been pulled from.

She recognized that she was going to be required to drink blood herself after her Ascension. It was a necessity to the existence of the necrids. She resolved that she never wanted to know where her blood was sourced from. Just blank, unlabeled vials. Let the lords debate what type of blood tasted the best; for her, it would only be about survival.

Once she confirmed the order was correct, she packed the boxes back up and was preparing to take them home when she felt a tug on her sleeve.

She turned and was faced with a raggedy young man, barely into his teens. His eyes were sunken, his skin was flushed, and his hair was wild. He had scars on his exposed arms. Puncture marks.

An escapee from the processing centers, she quickly realized.

"Please," he groaned. "They are coming... right behind me... I'm fast, I can outrun them... but I need a minute to catch my breath... please, just pull me into the shadows over there so I can hide... that's all I need... a minute to hide so I can catch my breath..."

Amaura felt sympathy for the boy, and the larger part of her heart wanted to do nothing more than to help him. Drag him into the shadows, stand watch for him, try to throw his pursuers off his track. But the logical part of her heart caused her instead to grab him, shove him to the ground, and pin his arm behind his back.

"Please, no..." he cried, weakly. "Why are you doing this... ? You are not one of them."

"I'm sorry, I wish I could pretend I didn't notice you," she replied, trying to keep her voice from cracking from grief. "But the moment you made contact with me, you sealed my fate and yours. I have a family, parents and a sister. If they found me helping you, all of us would wind up in the cages right next to yours. I do this for their sake."

Sure enough, she was barely finished speaking when the center enforcers burst onto the scene. She wasn't sure how much of their interaction they had seen, but she was confident she had made the right call. There was no way to save this boy. All she could do was ensure her family didn't suffer the same fate.

The escapee didn't resist when the enforcers grabbed him. He just went slack as tears streamed down his face. The enforcers muttered a quick word of thanks to Amaura before taking the boy away. Amaura repeated to herself in her head that she had done the only thing she could.

Amaura snapped back to reality, remembering that she couldn't be late. She grabbed the boxes and rushed toward her mistress's mansion.

"That was expedient work and I hear you were quite the hero." Talia, the matriarch of the Delmass clan, cooed her words of praise. "If only all of my slaves showed your degree of loyalty and hustle, our household would function with three times the efficiency."

Amaura was prostrating herself in front of her mistress, careful to keep herself respectfully still. "Thank you, mistress. It is a pleasure to serve."

"It is almost a shame that I will lose such a valuable slave after your ascension." Talia clicked her tongue. "But for every loss, there is a gain. I hope you will continue to serve our household with the same vigor in your new role as one of my administrators."

"Of course I will, mistress." Amaura tried hard not to smile, which could be viewed as a sign of disrespect. It was difficult not to smile when thinking about her new life as a citizen and not a slave. The quality of life she could give her family by taking them under her command. How her knees would never have to ache against the hard marble floor again.

"Rise, Amaura," her mistress commanded. "I want a better look at you."

Amaura did, careful to keep her eyes respectfully aimed down as she stood before her mistress. Talia was tall, slender, and menacing. Her ruby red lips seemed to bleed out from her snowy skin, and her white hair was like an icy river running down to her waist. Her eyes were red, bright as if they were aflame.

"Such striking feline features," Talia remarked. "No matter how many times I lay eyes on you, it compels me. It is why I took you as my own, back when you were but a child. And why I am so interested in seeing what you become. I don't believe my household has ever ascended one with your *unique* attributes. My curiosity about how those features will blend with those of the necrid is at its peak. What is the date of your Ascension again?"

"In two weeks' time, Mistress," Amaura answered. She was careful not to give an exact date in case things had been moved without her notice.

"Unacceptable, after such heroism today," Talia replied. "My interest is peaked and demands answers immediately. There is an Ascension scheduled today at the Ritual Hall for two other slaves of the household. I shall have you added as a third."

Amaura was so shocked she accidentally allowed herself to look her mistress in the eyes. "Today? As in, *today* today?"

Talia's expression was stony. "Is that a problem for you, Amaura?"

"No, of course not!" Amaura exclaimed, quickly looking back down towards the ground. "I'm just surprised—there's supposed to be some preparation, and I haven't gotten to tell my family—I am very grateful, though."

"I'm glad there isn't a problem," Talia interrupted her rambling. "Go and fetch your ritual robes and report immediately to the washroom to have your body made ready. If you're late for the ceremony, I can't promise when I will next give you this chance."

Amaura did not need to be told twice. She gave an appropriate bow, then quickly rushed through the estate towards the slaves' quarters.

Her Ascension was *today*! That was insane. Usually, slaves spent the week leading up to their Ascension resting and eating as much as they could to prepare their bodies for the process. Amaura was fairly confident in her fitness, but she had barely had any rest or food recently. How well her body would hold up was uncertain.

She put it out of her head. This was her time. There was no way, after all the beatings, abuse, and toil, that she would stop now.

Her only regret was not being able to tell her family the good news. They were scattered throughout the city performing their own duties this morning. She had wanted them there to observe her Ascension. She wondered how they would react when next they saw her and she was a necrid.

Thanks to her seniority, Amaura had her own corner in the slaves' quarters, which consisted of her own bed, a lantern on a post, and a small chest. She supposed she would get her own room, now. Maybe she could arrange for her sister to get her bed; then she would no longer have to share with their parents.

She popped open the chest and went digging for her ritual robes but couldn't find them. When was the last time she had worn them? The Halfmoon Ceremony? That was a month ago. Certainly, she got her robes back since then.

There wasn't time to ask around and see if they had been misplaced. Her mistress's tone had the ring of a threat to it: if she disappointed her mistress by not showing up on time to the Ascension, she would be forced to wait much longer for another chance.

Amaura did a quick double check that there was no one around, then raised her hand in front of her and called on the Tether.

From the stories she had heard from those born in foreign lands, people with a connection to the Tether like she had could use an object called a focus and specific hand and arm motions to do all kinds of fantastic and impressive things. That Amaura could call on the Tether at all without a focus spoke to a particularly rare affinity. Though all she could use it for were a few minor tricks, and those she had to practice in secret, as her mistress did not know of her ability. If this wasn't an emergency, she would never have dared while on estate grounds.

She steadied her breathing, focused her mind on an image of her ritual robes, and hoped they were nearby, as this spell did not have a particularly large range. The gestures were instinctual, as though her muscles moved on their own. There was a tug on her hand, as if someone had tied a string around her wrist and pulled. She followed the spell to where it led: the bed of one of her fellow slaves. Specifically, under the bed, where she found her robes.

Amaura had been aware that some slaves got jealous when one of them was about to ascend, but she never imagined that one would try to sabotage her. Well, no time to focus on that. She was just grateful that her Tether had allowed her to find it in time.

The Tether would be the thing she missed about this life the most. For a long time, she had hoped that when she was no longer a slave, she could finally obtain a focus and practice her magic in the open. Then she learned why she never saw any necrids using magic: they were incapable. For all the benefits the Ascension provided, it also cut a necrid completely off from the Tether.

It had always been there for her, like an old friend waiting to be called on. But she would have to sacrifice it in order to leave this life, and to make a better one for her family. A worthy sacrifice, but a painful one.

Tucking her robes under her arm, she quickly made her way to the washroom. There, two older men were waiting for her. They stripped her down and scrubbed her with a rough brush that felt more like it was trying to scrape off her skin than clean. They went over every inch of her body, taking so much time that Amaura worried they would make her late. When they finally finished, she quickly threw on her robes and raced to the Ritual Hall.

She barely made it. Everyone else was already inside, and the Turner was already standing in his place. Talia spotted her and nodded, then walked to the center of the room.

"The three of you gathered here today have proven a loyalty, competence, and uniqueness that stands above your peers. For this, you have been granted an opportunity to shed the skin of a slave and be reborn as a fellow necrid. As full members of Clan Delmass, you will be expected to conduct yourself with dignity, ferocity, and an unwavering devotion to expand our influence and power. It will not be easy. You will need to be re-educated to break the mindset of a slave. But you will come out of it not as a servant but as a master, if you survive the Ascension. Step forward now, prove your worth, and face your destiny."

An old man with silver hair stepped forward first. He walked with a limp and his hands were shaking. Amaura had seen him around. He had been waiting a very, very long time for this.

Six columns were positioned in a circle around the center of the room, and in front of each, a necrid in a white robe stood, chanting in a language Amaura did not know. She had only heard it spoken during ceremonies and was forbidden from asking about their meaning. She knew the Tether did not play any part in the ceremony, as necrids could not connect to the Tether, and always assumed it was an ancient custom.

The old slave steadied himself in front of the Turner, a massive necrid who loomed naked in front of them all, except for the chains binding his hands together in front of him and another that was looped around his neck, leashing him to the wall. The Turner snarled and growled, pulling on its chains in a desperate fervor to get closer to the man in front of it.

Talia glided to the wall that the Turner was leashed to and slowly, and slightly, loosened the chain.

The Turner lunged forward, using every extra inch it had been given to get its massive fangs around the neck of the old man. The slave howled in pain as blood burst from his neck, scattering across the floor and the face of the necrid.

"That's enough," Talia commanded as she heaved back on the chain.

The savage necrid resisted, but Talia's strength was too much as it was pulled back from the old man via the chain around its neck. The slave fell to the ground and his body convulsed. His body contorted unnaturally, spasms rapid and harsh, and Amaura swore she could hear the snapping of bone. After a minute, he went still.

Then he slowly rose. His skin had turned the pallid white of the masters. No longer did he look old and frail, and there was no shakiness to the way he held himself up any longer. He looked younger, stronger. He took a deep breath and let out a powerful howl.

"Welcome to the clan, brother," Talia declared as she approached him. She put a hand on his shoulder and lightly kissed his cheek. "Your new life begins now."

The newly born necrid saluted with a fist on his chest. "My existence belongs to Clan Delmass."

A young woman came next. The process was repeated, and again the Turner took a big bite out of the neck. But when the woman's spasms finally ceased, she did not rise. She lay still, crimson blood spilling from the gashing wound and forming a puddle around her.

"A failure," Talia declared with disgust. "Such a waste of good blood. One remains."

Talia grabbed the slain slave by the arm and roughly tossed her into a corner of the room as though tossing aside garbage, leaving a streak of blood behind her. Then she gestured for Amaura to step up.

Amaura's heart was beating out of her chest, and her every instinct told her to run. But there was no backing out of this now. She had to do this. This was her only chance to have a life outside of slavery.

She stepped up to the Turner and shut her eyes tight when she heard the chain being loosened. The pain of those fangs sinking into her flesh was far worse than she had imagined. It was as if she had been pierced by a dozen blades, after each blade had been frozen and its end made jagged. She was hardly aware of herself dropping to the ground as she lost control of her limbs.

She imagined herself falling backwards into a pool of ice water. The ice was in her veins, like jagged shards, snaking up her body until she wasn't sure where she ended and the frost began. Soon it would overtake her, and only the cold would remain.

Suddenly, there was also warmth. A trickle at first, melting through the ice and holding it at bay. It was a familiar warmth, something that had been with her as long as she could remember. The Tether.

A battle raged inside her, fire and ice. Then finally—stillness. The two forces were at equilibrium inside of her.

She opened her eyes and found herself back in the Ritual Hall, lying in the pool of blood the slave before her had left. She was still alive, which was a good sign. Did that mean she was finally a necrid? She felt different—lighter, mostly. But she expected she would feel the strength and virility of the necrids right away. Maybe it took some time to kick in.

Amaura pulled herself to her feet and looked around. Those gathered around her were looking at her with shock. And disgust.

No one's face was more twisted into a grimace than that of her mistress. Talia practically spat her next word, one which would dictate the course of Amaura's life from now on.

"Aborrent!"

Aborrent—a state not quite necrid, but not quite alive either, an incredibly rare outcome of the Ascension process. Everything a necrid got, she got a small portion of every aspect of a necrid: the enhanced power and vitality, the sensitivity to the sun, the blood thirst. Her hair and skin received the necrids' full bleached whiteness in the process.

But that was only physical. In the social order of Bloodstone, an Aborrent was worse than a slave. Most were taken away on the spot. It was only Talia's authority as the matriarch of the clan that had saved Amaura. "A pity to lose such a valuable slave. Return to your bed until I call for you."

Not that there wasn't a price to pay for this failure of her body. Her family—her parents and her sister—had been taken and thrown into the processing centers as her punishment. She never even had time to say goodbye or apologize for causing this to happen. In her despair, Amaura had tried to get herself taken as well, but now that her blood was partly mixed with necroplasm, she was not appetizing to the necrids, but she was valuable and could be traded to the necromancers to the south for spells and when magic was needed.

Everything after her family's imprisonment was hazy. Talia went on an impromptu trip out of the city and Amaura performed her duties without thought or feeling. It was as if her body acted on its own while her mind was locked in a cage. Slaves and Necrids hurled a torrent of abuse her way—she never anticipated missing "kitten," a far kinder moniker than "freak." So, she just continued on, because she didn't know what else to do.

The day came when Talia was set to return. Apparently, she was bringing back some important cargo, and Amaura was assigned to help unload. She didn't have any other duties that day, so she went to the dock early and waited. Waited for hours. Just staring off into the fog-covered sky.

The ship arrived, and Talia was the first to disembark. Amaura went through the motions of showing deference to her mistress. She knew her bows were getting sloppy, but what more could be done to her at this point?

"Amaura, dear, good, you're here," Talia said, her voice sing-song sweet. A rare good mood. "I've just made an important acquisition for our household, and she's going to need some breaking in. I'll need you to show her the ropes, as well as assist in her obedience training."

"Yes, mistress."

Talia put a hand under Amaura's chin and raised it so their eyes met. "Oh, don't be so upset, dear. I'm not replacing you. She's got a special purpose to fulfill, but you still have your role. After all, you may be a *freak* now, but you're my freak. And you will always belong to me."

"Yes, mistress." Her voice warbled. Something was welling up inside her.

The matriarch turned as Amaura struggled against the rising tears. Why now? This whole time since her failed Ascension, she hadn't cried. Not when she was declared an Aborrent, not when she was beaten for it, not when her family was taken. She had been numb. Why had what Talia said destroyed that shield of detachment?

This was bad. If she was caught showing this kind of emotion, her mistress might decide to get rid of her. She hated slaves who cried all the time. And without Talia's protection, she would be used in the blood banks as currency for the necromancers. She heard stories of how they would use the Aborrent blood in their gruesome experiments.

Someone stood in front of Amaura, positioned so that her face would be blocked from the view of the nearby necrids.

"Don't let them see you cry," the figure said. "You have to seem strong. Show them they can't break you."

The woman was a stark contrast to everything around her. She had tan skin, long, dark, wavy hair, confident brown eyes, and an athletic form. Her clothes, although torn, still had an elegance to them and she was covered in nicks and bruises, and yet there was still something noble about her posture and the way she spoke. It's as if she was radiating an aura that could pierce the perpetual dark.

But the chains around her wrists broke that illusion. However noble she might appear, she was a slave now and would soon have that nobility stripped from her.

Still, she was an usual sight, not the type of person they normally acquired from the slavers. She must have been someone wealthy, perhaps even someone important. No wonder Talia had gone to fetch her herself.

Curiosity, for the briefest moment, overwhelmed Amaura's sorrow. "How did someone like you wind up here?"

The new slave looked up at the dark, impenetrable sky. "How indeed."

Chapter 3

The sound of fighting echoed from below deck. The remaining drifters pulled up alongside the holes their weapons had bored into the side of the *Lord,* tethered to it via thick cables. More pirates crossed over those cables to invade the ship. For how small those ships were, there were a surprising number of invaders. The crew of the *Lord,* manned for peacetime and traveling through friendly skies, was not equipped for a battle of this scale. Tara knew the ship would be under the pirates' control soon.

Alarus seemed to have come to the same conclusion. "His majesty better not be putting any of the blame on me for losing his flagship. I wasn't even supposed to be on duty."

"We have to get to the bridge before the pirates do," Tara commanded.

"That's exactly where the attackers are going to be heading," Alarus said. "No, princess, I need to get you to the shuttle and away from here."

"The shuttle that's stored below deck. Where the pirates have boarded," she reminded him.

He scratched at his beard. "A fair point."

"The commander won't give up the ship without a fight, and I'm willing to gamble he will make his stand at the bridge. Our best chance is to join up with him."

Alarus sighed, defeated. "Ah, well. At least if we find Marzin, then this all becomes his responsibility. Stick close, and for once, try to show some restraint."

Unfortunately, they didn't get far. They had just entered the large main hallway that led up to the bridge when one door leading to the lower deck burst open. A rough-looking man came out into the passage, dressed in several layers of rough leathers and wielding a curved sword. That sword had recently been put to use, evidenced by the blood dripping from its blade.

His eyes fixed on them, and he pointed a finger. "Hey, your—!"

Before he could finish his thought, a swirl of sand appeared in front of his face and latched itself over his mouth, muffling him. The pirate struggled and tried to swat the sand away from him, but it kept swirling and when he tried to breathe or talk, sand rushed in.

"Shhh," Alarus whispered, his hand still gesturing as he controlled the flow of Tether to his spell. "It would be very rude for you to alert the others."

It wasn't enough, as the other pirates were already right behind him. Several more came filing out of the stairway. They quickly surrounded the princess and the mage, weapons drawn and ready—swords, daggers, even a couple of pistols!

"Alarus..." Tara whispered.

"Yes, I see them, princess," he mumbled. Then, to the pirates, "You feel good about yourselves, picking on a frail old man? Didn't you ever learn any manners?"

One pirate, a burly man wearing thick goggles, stepped to the front of the pack. "My apologies, respected elder. There is no reason for this to get physical. If you and the girl come quietly, I'll be sure you're handled with the gentlest of care."

"Oh, you promise?" Alarus's voice dripped with sarcasm. "Well, consider my worries abated."

Tara was crouched and ready, watching Alarus's lead. Waiting for an opportunity to run. Or to fight. Either way, she knew being captured was not an option.

An opportunity arose when the first pirate, who was still struggling with the sand around his face and had been stumbling about the passage, bumped into the goggled man. Goggles growled at him and shoved him.

Shoved him right towards Tara.

Tara seized the moment, jumping forward and grabbing the sword from the hand of the flailing pirate. She then slammed him with her shoulder, sending him back to impact against Goggles.

A flash of steel in her periphery. Tara whipped around and blocked the incoming sword with her own, drawing a gasp of surprise from the pirate wielding it.

Tara had never had to fight for her life before, but she had been training in many sword forms since she was a child. Court fencing taught to her by Master Moore so she could compete in the popular sport among the nobles. Southern Swift style mixed with the practical form of the military through the instructions of Marzin, in case she ever needed to defend herself. Styles out of Elondor and Lymeria, the basics of which she had learned from the reluctant knights and guards of visiting dignitaries.. She'd consider swordsmanship a hobby, a mix of refreshing exercise and a scholarly interest in the philosophy of each style.

She never imagined she would need to use it in a situation like this. The pirate brought his sword in for another swing, and Tara easily parried it. The pirate's technique was sloppy—aggressive with no thought for defense, and too low to get proper leverage on the swings. Immediately, Tara saw an opening, where she could run her sword right into his guts, but she couldn't take it. She wasn't ready to take a man's life, even a pirate's. But after turning aside another blow, she found another chance she could take. She slipped her sword underneath his and slashed up, cutting the pirate's hand open. Her opponent howled in pain, dropped his weapon, and stumbled back from her.

Tara wasn't given any time to celebrate her victory as a powerful arm grabbed her from behind. It wrapped tight around her and pinned her sword arm to her side. She struggled and tried to remember what she was taught about breaking holds. It was much harder to think in actual combat than in practice.

A click right beside her head. She looked over and saw that Goggles had his pistol pressed right up against her.

"That's enough of that," he said. "You don't want to make a big mess for us to clean up, do you?"

He took the sword from her, then motioned for the large man holding her to let her go. There was an infuriating grin on his face.

"That's better, isn't it?" he said.

Then he smacked her across the side of the face with his pistol. Tara saw stars and felt herself falling to the ground.

"Princess!" Alarus called out. He seemed to ready another spell based on his hand gestures, but before he could finish it, another of the pirates hit him in the back of the head with a sap. He groaned and collapsed to the floor right next to her.

"Pity we're not supposed to rough her up too bad," Goggles said.

"Bitch, cut my hand."

Goggles grinned. "Well, maybe we can rough her up just a little more."

The door behind them swung open, and the pirates were stunned by a shout of anger and a flash of steel.

Tara had seen Marzin fight before when giving demonstrations or in friendly competitions with other members of the royal guards. She'd seen him spar when helping train the troops, watched him practice his sword forms, and even been on the receiving end of quite a few blows from him when he would show her the weaknesses in her defenses during their lessons. But she had never seen him in actual combat before.

Now she knew all the stories about him were not mere exaggeration.

Two of the pirates had already received fatal cuts across their midsections before they were even aware of what was happening. Another attempted to stab Marzin with his knife, but lost the knife, along with his entire hand, in a single swing. The large man tried to grab Marzin from behind, but found he was not as easy to pin as Tara had been. Marzin slammed his elbow into his assailant's ribs, and then again into his face. As the pirate stumbled back, Marzin thrust his sword backwards, impaling the pirate.

The remaining pirates attempted to circle Marzin and attack him all at once. He did not leave them a single opening, batting away each strike like a horse swatting flies. His sword moved through the air so fast the pirates were the ones who seemed outnumbered. When one pirate slipped on the blood that was pooling on the floor, it was over for them. Marzin thrust through the pirate's exposed chest. The others around him tried to back away in horror, leaving them open to fatal strikes of their own.

Goggles was the last one standing. He had backed away as soon as the fighting started and had been trying to line up a shot at Marzin with his pistol. His hand was shaking now after seeing what the commander was capable of. "You—how did you—!?"

Marzin cleared the gap between them in two steps. Goggles fired. Marzin swung.

Tara's eyes failed to track the action to tell if Marzin had somehow deflected the bullet with his sword or if Goggles had simply missed, but when everything was settled, Goggles was on the ground and Marzin was untouched.

The commander helped a wide-eyed Tara back to her feet. "Are you alright, princess?"

She rubbed at the swelling side of her face. "I think my pride is hurt worse than my body. How come you never taught me to fight like that?"

Marzin looked back at the dead and dying pirates on the ground. "You know the forms, but applying them this way only comes from experience. I pray you never see enough combat to do what I can."

They went to check on Alarus, who had yet to stir. His hair was colored red where he had been hit, but he was still breathing. It was hard to tell when, or if, he would regain consciousness.

"Well, that's not ideal," Marzin commented. "With him out of the action, the only one on this ship able to pilot the shuttle is Captain Denbar. If he's even still alive—I can feel that the ship has already moved off course, meaning the boarders must have taken the bridge."

"Then we have no choice but to head towards the bridge," Tara declared. "Either we find and extract the captain, or we retake control of the *Lord*. Personally, I'm hoping for the latter."

Marzin nodded. "I don't know what's gotten these pirates so emboldened that they dare to attack the kingdom's flagship, but I intend to teach them a lesson about Rainecourt swordsmanship. Follow and stay close."

Tara slung Alarus's arm around her shoulder and hoisted him up. Fortunately, the Kray was pretty light. She carried him as she followed behind Marzin down the passage, up the access stairs, and straight to the bridge.

The state of the bridge was a disturbing sight. The crew manning the bridge had been slain, their bodies slumped over the various instruments—all save for Captain Denbar, who was being watched over by a group of pirates. His head was hung in shame, though no one could blame him for losing control of the bridge against these kinds of odds. The pirates were prying open panels for some reason—did they think something was hidden here?

The man in the center unmistakably commanded this band of murderers. His coat was adorned with all manner of buttons and buckles, arranged in a chaotic jumble, as if to intentionally mock the badges and insignias displayed on the uniforms of military officers. He wore a tricorn hat, from which several long braids protruded, and thick, darkly tinted spectacles.

Before Marzin could even open the door to the bridge, the pirate captain was already grinning towards him. "Come on in, now. Don't be shy. I've been expecting you. I'm glad to see you are unharmed."

Marzin frowned. "So much for any element of surprise. Stay back and let me handle it."

Tara crouched beside the doorway as Marzin strode inside. The pirates watched as he approached their leader, but no one made a move towards him.

"Commander Marzin," the pirate captain said, sounding genuinely pleased. "I'm glad you have lost none of your talent. This would have been much more boring if you had died before we even chatted. We have so much to catch up on, after all."

Marzin scrutinized the pirates scattered throughout the bridge, careful to be ready if they tried to surround him. "Catch up? Don't recall meeting many pirates. At least, not any who have lived to tell the tale."

"Oh, come on, Galvin. It hasn't been that long, has it?" The pirate lifted the spectacles from his face. "Have you truly forgotten me?"

The commander's face dropped. "Darrian? You're—you're alive?"

Darrian? Where had Tara heard that name before? It echoed faintly in her memory.

"That's Captain Blake to you, now," Darrian said with a laugh. "You're not the only one earning fancy titles. But I am glad you finally remember me."

"The titles of an outlaw are worth less than dirt," Marzin spat. "What are you doing here, Darrian? How could you betray the crown like this?"

"Me, betray? Oh, no, my old friend, I think you have that backwards." Darrian looked over to the doorway where Tara was hiding. "Did he ever tell you about me, princess? I was this close to being one of the royal guards tasked with your protection as well. Galvin selected me out of all the recruits to train personally. He taught me the sword, took me out into combat to experience wetting my blade, taught me about court life and honor and all that bullshit. For a young, impressionable lad like myself, he was almost like a father. But I guess he didn't feel quite the same bond for me, since he had no problem leaving me to die."

That was it. Tara remembered hearing that Marzin had taken an apprentice named Darrian. He had died, and Marzin was so torn up about it he never took another. He seemed less dead than Marzin had thought.

"That's not what happened," Marzin insisted.

"Isn't it? I seem to remember it quite clearly. We were assigned to clear out that pirate base, and you told me afterwards you would officially give me the badge of the royal guard. I was so eager. But the pirates put up a bigger fight than we were expecting, and a retreat was called. You and I were supposed to hold the line, buy time for the rest of our soldiers to clear out. A valiant stand, you might say. But while I stood, you ran away, leaving poor little me to fend off those pirates on my lonesome."

Marzin grimaced. "You took a bolt to the chest and fell; I saw it. Unable to hold that passage any longer alone, I fell back. I had no idea you were still alive!"

"Never even bothered to check." Darrian tsked. "If you had, you would have seen that my armor took the brunt of that bolt, and only an inch pierced into me. I got back on my feet and found myself alone. How disappointed I was. Ah, but there is no reason to keep dredging up the past. I did pretty well for myself afterwards. After I was captured, I proved myself to the pirates, was invited to join them, and then even rose through the ranks of their leadership. And look at me now! Captain of my very own fleet! You should be proud."

"Proud that you would turn your blade against your own people!" Marzin exclaimed. "I understand your grudge against me. It is justified. But how can you lead an attack against Rainecourt like this?"

"Oh, but it is because of my grudge against you I did." Darrian sounded all too happy to reply. "I almost turned this job down, you know? Too messy, too many risks, too much of a chance that I'll have the entire Rainecourt Navy on my ass afterwards. But then I heard you were going to be here, and how could I refuse the opportunity to say hi to an old friend? I just wanted you to know—whatever has happened here, and everything that will happen, is all your fault."

"The only one to blame here is the traitor in front of me." Marzin pointed his sword at the pirate captain.

"Then let's settle this, shall we? Just you and me." Darrian drew his own blade. "If you win, my men will abandon this ship without further fuss. But if I win—well, you don't want to know what's planned for your precious princess."

Tara clutched the edge of the doorframe. This Darrian character sounded confident, but she had faith in Marzin's swordsmanship. Whether the other pirates would honor his word once he was defeated remained to be seen, but it was as good of a chance as they were going to get.

The two circled each other, their steps deliberate and careful. The first clashes of their blades were cautious, slow and light, attacks meant not to hit but to probe. They were testing each other, getting a sense of each other's form and reach.

Then all at once, they burst into action, swords clashing at such a speed that Tara could hardly keep up. It was clear at once that Darrian was a master of his craft. He moved with a lethal efficiency and a well-practiced polish. When paired against Marzin, the two seemed to be locked more in a dance than a fight, their styles complementing one another as they built up a deadly rhythm.

But as good as Darrian was, Marzin was better. He was always one step ahead in their dance, his sword edging ever closer to finding a mark on his opponent with each passing exchange. Darrian was showing signs of getting winded. It was only a matter of time before his defense slipped.

"You were always talented, Darrian," Marzin growled as their swords pressed together. "You would have made an exceptional royal knight."

"Eh, being a pirate is a lot more fun!"

They exchanged strikes once more, and Marzin turned Darrian's blade away with his own, then shouldered the pirate backwards. Darrian's back hit the helm, and his sword arm went wide. He was vulnerable. Marzin stepped in to deliver the decisive strike.

A loud *bang* erupted throughout the bridge. Marzin stopped in his tracks, sword still raised to make the killing blow. Time seemed to freeze.

Then the sword dropped from Marzin's hand, and the commander fell to his knees.

It took Tara a minute to piece together what had happened. Then she saw the smoke rising from under the sleeve of Darrian's off-hand, and when he raised his arm to let the sleeve recede from his hand, it confirmed her suspicion. He had been concealing a pistol under his sleeve the entire time.

"A damn shame," Darrian said, his voice joyous. "I thought in your old age, you'd slow down enough that I could beat you in a fair duel, but you're just as fast as you ever were. Unfortunately, you're also just as foolish. You really thought I would fight fair? This is just like when you took part in the Corbinite Trials—one dirty trick is all it takes to take you out. Except this time, no bracelet is going to save you."

"Princess..." Marzin struggled to say, but his voice was ragged. "I..."

Darrian removed Marzin's head from his shoulders. Tara couldn't help but scream as the head of the commander of the royal guard rolled towards her.

"Not everyone deserves last words." The pirate looked over at the door with a grin. "Now, to claim my prize."

He took a step forward—

A hand composed of rock appeared around his throat. Another gripped his sword arm and pinned it to his side. A third appeared behind him and pressed its palm flat against his back. From the grunt of pain it elicited, it must have been pressing down hard.

Alarus was back on his feet, and despite his injury, his eyes were fixed and determined, hardened by grief. "None of you move. If one of you takes even one step towards the princess, I'll snap your captain's spine like it's a twig. Believe me, I really want to, so don't test me. Captain Denbar! Get the princess to the shuttle and get away from here!" The glow of the glyph in front of his hands echoed across the sweat on his face.

The naval captain's lizard-like eyes darted around to the surrounding pirates. None of them seemed to move to stop him. He nodded and started walking towards the door.

"Alarus..." Tara whispered.

"I know, princess, I chose a hell of a time to take my duty to the royal family seriously," the mage replied, his attention still focused on the target of his spell. "Maybe that hit to the back of my head knocked something loose. Just go with Denbar and get out of here."

Denbar moved carefully through the bridge, watching the surrounding pirates. The threat against the captain was working, as none of them dared to move. Darrian continued to groan in pain as the earthen hands pressed up against him.

He got to the door, where Alarus was standing firm, and stepped as if to pass beside him.

Instead, he plunged a knife into Alarus's chest.

The old mage was so stunned, it seemed to take him a moment to realize he had been stabbed. Finally, he dropped his arms. The spell's glyph faded, releasing the spell, and he clutched at the knife in his chest.

"Oh," was all he could say before collapsing to the ground.

Tara put a hand over her mouth to conceal her horror. "Captain Denbar! What have you done!?"

Denbar looked away from her, and Tara realized that the shame she had seen in his eyes earlier was not for surrendering the bridge—it was because he was aligned with the pirates all along!

"I'm sorry, princess," Denbar mumbled. "Money has always been a concern of mine, and I'm in a position now where I need a lot. More than the royal family will offer to repay. The pirates are going to clear my debt, and then some. I didn't have a choice."

"Have you sunk so low you can put a price on the lives of your comrades?" Tara shouted. "The people you've fought beside for years!"

Denbar looked at the corpse he had just created. "I suppose I can."

"Don't be too harsh on him, princess." Darrian rubbed at his throat, but being strangled and nearly having his spine broken didn't seem to hurt his mood. "It is *a lot* of money. I'm almost jealous. I don't think there is anyone out there that would put such an enormous price on *me*. What's a guy got to do to get noticed?"

Tara steeled her resolve and raised her chin. There was no escaping now, and she couldn't fight them. But she was still a princess of Rainecourt, and she would still act like it, no matter what these pirates had in store for her.

"Who put a price on me?" Tara asked, trying to sound commanding.

Darrian smiled at her. "Have you ever been to Bloodstone?"

Chapter 4

The dizziness struck again. Amaura tried to right herself against the wall to maintain her balance, but her hand slipped and she once again found herself on her hands and knees. Her breath came in sharp bursts and she struggled to stop the world from spinning around her.

It would pass, she knew. It always passed. But these episodes were becoming more frequent. How much longer could she keep this up? Should she even try?

One solution existed to quell the weakness and exhaustion plaguing her for weeks. But she found even the thought repulsive.

As a certain pair of ornate shoes came into her view, she realized the choice might no longer be hers.

"I don't recall assigning you to clean the floors today," Talia stated. "In fact, I believe you are supposed to be heading down to the cells to care for my acquisition."

"I'm sorry, mistress," Amaura said, finally finding the strength to get to her feet. "I'm on my way down."

The matriarch looked Amaura in the eyes, seeming to stare into her soul. "You look weak. Have you been drinking the blood I have allotted to you?"

"Yes, Mistress," Amaura lied.

Talia had locked in on her problem immediately. Despite the matriarch allotting her a small amount of blood once a week to go with her rations, Amaura could not bring herself to drink any of it. She had always known that Ascension would mean being required to drink blood to sustain herself, but she had always planned to close her eyes and not think about where that blood was being sourced from. Now, she couldn't help but think about it. Her family was in the processing centers. What were the odds that the blood she was served was drained right from the veins of her sister? Even if it was a slight chance, she couldn't bring herself to drink it.

Technically, Aborrents didn't need to drink blood to survive, in the way necrids did. But to avoid growing weak, they occasionally needed to drink some blood. Amaura had hoped if she just bore with it, she would eventually get used to the feeling of weakness and be able to overcome it. However, simplicity eluded her, and daily tasks became more challenging.

She was worried that if Talia learned she wasn't drinking the provided blood, her mistress would use force to ensure she did. Followed by a severe punishment for defying her orders and wasting the generosity of her mistress.

"I'm just a little under the weather," Amaura said, trying to keep her dishonesty from her voice. "Us Aborrents don't inherit the perfect health of true necrids. We're still susceptible to the common chill."

Amaura had a reputation for honesty. She hoped that would carry her through this obvious deception.

"I see." Talia's voice gave no sign of whether or not she believed her. "Well, ill or not, you have duties to see to. Once they are complete, you can spend the rest of the day resting if you wish."

"Thank you, mistress."

"And if you need an additional portion of blood, do let me know," Talia added. "I recognize that keeping you in your current 'condition' comes with some additional costs. Costs I am willing to pay so long as you keep proving yourself worth it."

"Of course, mistress. I am eternally grateful for your generosity." Amaura knew she should bow while saying that, but she was worried if she tried that right now, she would fall over.

If the matriarch noticed the disrespect, she didn't show it. She nodded and continued on her way, enough of her time already wasted on this one slave.

Amaura let out a sigh of relief. She didn't know how long she could keep this condition a secret. Assuming Talia didn't already realize and was just choosing not to do anything about it yet. It is possible she was giving her more rope to hang herself with by allowing her to carry on lying. But all she could think about was delaying drinking that blood as long as she could.

Right now, getting her daily tasks done while she had the energy was the priority.

The cells always gave her a sense of dread when she was forced to go down there. It was the one duty she was always trying to trade with her fellow slaves, even if it meant exchanging for longer and more arduous tasks. No one was willing to trade with her anymore. Few were even willing to speak with her anymore. Such was the fate of an Aborrent.

It was sort of strange that she had such an aversion to it, having spent no time behind those bars herself. She was born in Bloodstone, and in her earliest memories, she was already being put through education. Only acquisitions spent time in the cells, and only the ones who displayed too much independence and defiance to be properly educated. Down there, they would be subjected to all manner of terrible things until their spirits were broken enough that their education could begin. She'd seen many people go down into a cell, from muscular soldiers to prideful scholars, and while some took longer than others, all eventually came out the same.

She didn't think it was sympathy that gave her that feeling of unease in the cells. As far as she was concerned, the acquisitions were just making it hard on themselves by not complying more readily. The sooner they accepted their fates, the sooner they could begin working towards additional privileges, and if they played the game right, they could even become a necrid lord themselves. Unless they wound up like Amaura, anyway.

Maybe it was the thought of her parents down here. They didn't like to talk about their past before being acquired by the Delmass clan. Well, more like they were forbidden to. All Amaura knew was that they came from some place warm in the far west, were taken to Bloodstone when they were young, and spent some time in the cells before their education. The thought of them enduring the horrors of the cells was upsetting.

Though they were enduring far worse now.

Amaura couldn't let herself get lost thinking about that now. If she did, she would not be able to function. Just focus on the work.

There was only one person occupying the cells right now. The same noble woman whom Amaura had met at the docks weeks past. Her name was Tara, and apparently she was an even bigger deal in her home country than Amaura had first thought. She wasn't sure what position Tara held, but she had deduced some connection to royalty.

An unusually important person to be taken by the Delmass clan. Mistress Talia must have had some plans for her.

Tara's kindness was clear to Amaura. She could tell she was a kind girl. That much had been apparent from their first meeting, when she had shielded Amaura's tears from public view. Since then, she had continued to treat Amaura with respect and kindness during their encounters. Amaura had sincerely hoped and even advised Tara to accept her situation quickly to avoid the worst of the treatment.

Unfortunately, based on the bruises on Tara's face and the bloody bandage wrapped around her leg, it appeared she had not heeded Amaura's advice.

"Amaura, it is nice to see you again," Tara said. She winced as she stood and put weight on her injured leg. "When I heard you coming, I thought you were those bruisers coming back for another round. I have a few choice words for them, but perhaps after I've had a moment to heal. Is it supper time already?"

"If you can call it that," Amaura replied, dropping the small satchel in front of her. "Bread, water, and some discards from the kitchen that might have once been vegetables. I tried to sneak in some of the slaves' rations again, but they have been watching me closely."

Tara took the food without complaint. "It was nice while it lasted. Though I feel like I could deal with nothing but bread and rot, if only I could get a hot cup of tea down here. The mistress here has a lot to learn about hosting guests."

"I wouldn't take it too personally," Amaura said. "I've been serving her my whole life, and I've never seen a cup of tea myself."

"Well, that is quite improper. Tea is a universal right." Tara said with vigor, although the wince of pain after may have ruined the moment.

"Maybe after you've officially joined the household, you can bring that up. Work hard, become a favored slave, and for your privilege, ask for a cup of tea to be added to slaves' daily rations."

Tara took a big bite out of the hard bread. "Well, that is very tempting, but I'm afraid I still must decline joining the Delmass clan at this time."

Amaura sighed. "I was afraid you were going to say that. They're not going to stop, you know? The more you resist, the worse things they're going to do."

"I know. But I'm carrying my family's pride and dignity. I would never disgrace that by allowing myself to be reduced to a slave. No offense meant to present company."

"None taken." Amaura lifted her arm to show off her pale skin. "I myself was about to be made a lord. I can't imagine I would have let anything take that away from me if I had succeeded."

Tara looked at her curiously. "What happened?"

"It didn't stick."

Amaura went through her duties—checking the condition of the prisoner, cleaning the cell, ensuring the security of the cell. She noticed that one of the locks on the door seemed to be jammed. Seemed to be. It appeared the mistress's men were up to one of their more nefarious tricks. She struggled with whether she should warn Tara about it. Being friendly with Tara and sneaking her extra food was one thing; interfering with the breaking process was another. Amaura would be in serious trouble if Talia found out.

Another wave of dizziness came on her then and Amaura found herself forced to take a seat right next to the cell. They were getting so close together. This could not continue.

"Are you alright?" Tara asked. "You look more beaten down than me."

"Just need a moment," Amaura replied.

"I thought necrids didn't get sick," Tara inquired.

"But I'm only half of one. And it's that half that's bringing me down. I need to drink blood to keep my strength up—but I can't. I simply can't bring myself to, knowing how they get it."

Amaura didn't know why she was confessing this to Tara. It was foolish. If Tara told her captors, that would be it for Amaura. But even though Tara was a prisoner and Amaura was part of the household keeping her there, she felt Tara could be trusted.

"I see. Well, it won't do for you to grow too weak to do your work. The next person they send to care for me might not be quite as good at making conversation. Hand me that bread knife. Let's do this quickly." Tara reached out her hand through the bars of her cell.

"Huh? What are you—?"

"You need blood. I'll give you some of mine." Tara spoke in a matter-of-fact way.

Amaura was caught off guard. "You—that's not necessary."

"As long as you don't need more than I can spare, I don't see the issue," Tara argued. "You can't drink the blood they give you because it is being taken from unwilling victims, yes? Well, I am willingly giving you some of mine. Now don't be ungrateful."

As confused as she was about the situation, Amaura still ended up complying with the prisoner's demand and handed her the bread knife. It wasn't until the knife was already in Tara's hand that Amaura realized that giving her a potential weapon was a violation of at least a dozen rules.

Fortunately, Tara was true to her word. She cut her finger and allowed a small trickle of blood to drip into her empty water cup. When a small pool had formed at the bottom of the cup, she handed the cup and the knife back to Amaura.

"I hope that's enough," Tara said. "Any more than that and I might start to get woozy myself."

Amaura held the cup for a while, looking at the precious red liquid it contained. She had many reservations, but ultimately could not contain her desire. For the first time since her failed Ascension, Amaura drank blood.

Tara's blood tasted fruity and slightly sweet. It was very pleasant, and not at all what Amaura had been expecting. She thought back to the menu at the blood bank and wondered if Tara's blood would have gone for a special price for being from nobility.

Almost immediately, Amaura began to feel the effects. Her strength returned, her vision sharpened, and her mind cleared. It was as if she had been living under a heavy fog that had all at once been lifted. She didn't know the last time she felt this strong.

"Thank you, Tara. I don't know how to repay you."

Tara waved a hand dismissively. "Don't mention it. I have a duty to care for others."

"Still, I wish there was something I could do for you." At that moment, Amaura made a decision. "Tara, have you noticed that one of the locks in this door is jammed?"

Tara didn't respond, but she did look purposefully away from the door. *She had noticed.*

"It's part of a trap," Amaura explained. "One I've seen them do many times before. Some of your torturers will deliberately let you see how they open the entrance to the tunnel that goes outside. Once they are sure you have seen it, they will jam the lock on the door. They want you to think you have a chance to escape. The point is to let you have a glimmer of hope so that it is more painful when they tear it down. You will reach the end of the tunnel, but just as you are coming into the fresh air, you'll be grabbed by a group of slave catchers who were waiting there for you. They'll beat you and throw you right back in the cell. Don't fall for it."

"Is that right?" Tara sounded a bit disappointed, but not concerned. "That's a pretty clever trap. I can see how having your hopes dashed like that could get to some people."

"Your best course is to pretend like you haven't noticed the jammed lock."

"I will keep that in mind. Thank you, Amaura."

As Amaura left the cells, she came to a realization about why she dreaded coming down here so much. Tara's kindness made it all the clearer: this was a place where humanity was drained. People went in, and the empty vessels drained of their souls came out.

And worse, it reminded Amaura that she had never had that humanity to begin with. She had been born a slave, lived her life as a slave, and would die as a slave.

She never had a soul to lose.

The chill had returned to Bloodstone. As a consequence of blocking out most of the daylight, when the cold wind swept down from the north shores, there was little of the sun's warmth to dissipate them. The cold just lingered there, for weeks at a time, seeping into everything.

For the necrids, this bothered them little. They couldn't feel the chill. In fact, they needed to be careful when it got truly frigid because they could get frostbitten on their extremities without even noticing. For the slaves, the chill meant bundling up in as many layers as they could. They weren't afforded any particularly thick clothing, so they'd often wear every piece they owned to give them some protection.

As was becoming routine, much of Amaura's clothing had been missing from her trunk this morning. She didn't know whether it was one of her fellow slaves or a necrid of the household doing this to her. Both seemed to despise her equally these days. Unfortunately, she did not inherit much of the necrid resistance to the cold in her state as an Aborrent, so as she made her way down the streets in only what she could find, she felt the chill biting into her bones.

All she could do was try to get her mistress's business done as quickly as possible. First to the Hall of Records to drop off a scroll. The minister there gave Amaura a hard time about the contents of the scroll, despite the fact that it was in a language she couldn't read and she had been given no details on its contents. Then onto the port to help with loading the mistress's ship for its next trip. And finally, a quick stop at the library to grab a book that Talia requested.

On a whim, she gambled on telling a lie to the librarian and claimed that her mistress required two books. In addition to the book on ancient languages that she was sent to fetch, she also asked for a book on Rainecourt. Tara's homeland.

She was curious if she could learn more about Tara by studying a book on her home. Maybe she could even learn what Tara's connection to their royal family was. Tara was quite the curious person, and Amaura's curiosity was getting the best of her.

The librarian didn't question her, thankfully, and she was able to quickly make her way back to the Delmass Estate.

She'd hoped it would be warm inside, but unfortunately it seemed no one had gotten a fire going in the slaves' quarters yet. The rest of her peers must still be out on other errands. Nobody had left any fire starters near the fireplace, either.

Amaura looked around carefully to be extra sure that there was truly no one around, then put her hands before the fireplace, focused, and channeled the Tether. A sigil formed in the air in front of her fingertips, the one she had come to associate with fire. A small series of sparks sprinkled over the fireplace, nothing impressive but enough to light the wood inside. Soon a small fire was burning, its blessed warmth cutting through the miserable chill.

If there was a single silver lining to be taken from her failed Ascension, it was that she had not lost her connection to the Tether as a necrid would have. Its presence was a comfort, one consistency left over from her life before everything went terribly wrong. She still had to be careful not to be caught using it. People had enough problems with her just for being an Aborrent.

With a little bit of free time to her name, she found a comfortable spot in front of the fire and took out the book on Rainecourt. She learned about the capital city Aurelia's Hold named for King Aurelius Rainecourt, a city built with Steam-Tek and Magi-Tek, a mix of magic and steam technology advancements shared from their allies. Massive towers that reached out into the sky and a mixture of architecture that stretched back generations to recent times. She read how it was a land where peoples of various races could live and all were considered equal under the law. It was a kingdom where slavery was outlawed. Most interesting to her were the bits about the Maxwell Klyne Sentinel Academy, a prestigious military academy renowned for producing some of the best soldiers on the continent, and the Tine Academy of Magical Arts, where those with a connection to the Tether could learn how to better control it and use a focus. She wondered if, had she been born in Rainecourt, she could have been accepted into a school like that. She'd prefer to learn more about the Tether, but military strategy could be interesting as well.

She nearly dropped the book when she came to the section on the royal family. The first page showed King Davies Rainecourt. Above a description of his reign was a portrait of a handsome man with a golden beard the same color as his elaborate crown. But what shocked Amaura was what was on the opposing page—Tara Rainecourt, princess!

In the portrait, she was still only a child. Couldn't have been more than five or six years old. But there was no question with those eyes that this was the same Tara they currently had in the cells. Tara wasn't just connected to royalty, she was the daughter of the king and heir to the throne!

What was Talia thinking? Was she trying to start a war with Rainecourt? No, she was too careful. It was likely she had covered her tracks well enough that Tara's family didn't know where she was. But what was the purpose of kidnapping a princess and trying to turn her into a slave? Knowing the mistress, she had plans. And they were unlikely to be pleasant.

"Amaura, a word?" a gruff male voice called out.

Amaura startled and quickly tossed the book behind her, barely missing the fireplace. She got carelessly absorbed in the book and hadn't noticed anyone arrive.

The Delmass clan's chief torturer, Vents, stood impatiently at the door to the slaves' quarters. He was bald, an unusual choice for a necrid, and that bare forehead wrinkled when he was angry. And he was always angry.

"Did you hear me calling, Amaura?" Vents asked.

She got to her feet quickly to bow before the torturer. "I'm sorry, sir. What can I help you with?"

"I've been assigned to dealing with our current guest in the cells," he explained. "I understand you have been spending quite a bit of time down there with her."

Amaura was frozen. What had he heard? Was he about to punish her for interfering with her torture?

"I've been regularly assigned to her care these past few weeks," Amaura replied, trying to keep the nerves from her voice. "No one else seems to want to do it."

He nodded as if he expected that answer. "Have you learned anything about her during that time?"

"Sir?" she asked, confused.

Vents's expression softened. "I'll admit that this woman has proven tougher to break than usual, and the mistress is growing impatient for results. She even fell into the 'fake escape' trap, and it hasn't seemed to have much of an impact on her. So, I'm wondering if you have learned anything about her during your time in the cells? Anything you can think of, even if it doesn't sound important, might give me an idea on how to better proceed."

She fell into that trap? But Amaura had warned her specifically about it. Why would she still walk into it?

"I'm not sure..." Amaura started.

"I know you've had a tough time since becoming an Aborrent," Vents continued. "If you help me, I can help you. I have an open position—easy work that needs to be done behind the scenes. It comes with privileges and a great deal of independence. The mistress will not deny me if I ask to put you in that position."

Amaura's eyes went to the book lying beside the fireplace. It was full of information on Tara's homeland and family. It would easily qualify for what Vents was looking for.

Normally, Amaura wouldn't hesitate for an opportunity like this. Something simple she could do to get in the good graces of someone high in the clan, that granted her easier assignments and more privileges? That was an easy choice, one that anyone in her position would quickly take.

And yet she couldn't. Not if it had a chance of hurting Tara further.

"Sorry, sir. If I had something, I would tell you," she lied. "I don't really talk much when I'm down there. I just drop off her food, clean her cell, and leave as quickly as I can."

Vents frowned, but it didn't seem like he doubted her. "That's unfortunate. Well, the offer stands. If you get her to say something about herself during your time down there, I'll make it worth your while."

"That's very generous, sir. Thank you."

She waited till Vents left and was far out of sight before starting to make her way towards the cells. Until she was safely in the passage leading down into the cells, she kept an eye out to make sure no one was paying attention to her. She didn't want to answer why she was going to the cells when she wasn't assigned there today.

Tara looked worse than ever. The slave catchers had not been gentle with her. She looked at Amaura with the one eye she was capable of opening.

"Amaura... I didn't expect your company today," she said, weakly.

"Are you stupid?!" Amaura near-shouted. "I warned you about the trap! Why did you still try to escape?"

"If I hadn't, they might have figured out who had warned me about the trap," Tara said. "I'd hate for you to get into trouble on my account. Besides, even if it was a setup, I still couldn't help but take my chances. It beats sitting around doing nothing. I had sort of hoped that being aware that it was a trap would help me overcome it. That obviously did not work out. Damn, those necrids are strong."

Amaura put her face in her hands. "You're so reckless. And I'm... I'm so useless. I tried to help you just one time and I still couldn't do anything for you."

"Not yet. But I refuse to give up." Tara closed her eyes, rested against the back of her cell, and let out a painful sigh. "An opportunity will come. I believe that. I just have to last until then. That opportunity might require your help. I hope you will be willing then."

"Whatever I can do," Amaura promised.

"If only that grumpy old wizard was here with me," Tara said, wistfully. "He'd just wave his hands, send a message home. They'd have a rescue ready in no time."

"Send a message?" Amaura asked. "You mean like... with the Tether?"

Tara's good eye opened slightly. "I'm surprised you heard of it. I thought there were no mages in Bloodstone. Yes, the Tether could be used to send messages over vast distances. The court wizard, may he rest in peace, was always sending and collecting status reports from throughout the kingdom. He said all you had to do was have a clear image of the person you wanted to send the message to in your mind, channel the Tether, and then speak the words while doing the gestures."

She imitated the gestures with her hand. "Unfortunately, I don't have a real connection to the Tether myself," Tara said with a sigh. "I've seen the spell performed so many times I can copy the gestures closely, but even if I had a focus, I could never perform the magic myself."

Amaura was excited to learn about another application of the Tether she had never considered before. And even more, she was happy to have an idea of how she might be able to help Tara.

"I've got to go, but I'll be back in a little bit," Amaura said. "Hang in there."

"I'm not going anywhere," Tara replied.

Amaura returned to the slaves' quarters and picked up the book she had discarded. She flipped back to the page with the portrait of the king. The portrait was a couple of decades out of date, but hopefully it was still close enough for the spell.

She concentrated on envisioning him in her mind as clearly as she could, then pulled the Tether to her. She imitated the gestures Tara had shown her with her hand. It was a strange pattern, but it felt right. Pure instinct had driven every use of her Tether that she had discovered , but this was different. This felt like she was shaping it, in a way. Not just acting as its conduit, but as its master.

As the power swelled, she whispered the words, "Your daughter is in Bloodstone, in the cells beneath the Delmass Estate. You must hurry—I know not how much time she has left."

An unfamiliar sigil appeared in front of her hands. It formed two concentric circles which rotated in opposite directions. The words appeared upon the spokes of the circles. The circles spun faster as the last word was spoken. Then suddenly disappeared.

The power faded. Was the spell successful? How would she even know?

There was no response. She didn't know if there was supposed to be.

All she could do was hope that the message had reached its destination. And that it was not too late.

Chapter 5

It had been fifteen years since the last time Grayson was in the capital Aurelia's Hold. The last time he had seen these great towers and the giant clouds of steam they exhausted, he had been but a boy. As he stood on the prow of the airship *Outrider* and took in the sights of the city below him, he felt much the same boyish wonder he felt back then.

The city was laid out in overlapping circles. Grayson had been taught that the circles were laid out in a way that had some kind of arcane significance, although his understanding of magic started and stopped with the tools of his trade and the quickest way to put a bullet through the eyes of someone trying to channel the Tether. Whatever the purpose of the layout was, it created a visual layering, as if witnessing multiple cities that had somehow come to rest on each other's shoulders.

The highest of these circles hosted the docking towers for the airships. It was early in the day, during the peak traffic hours, and half a dozen of ships swarmed around the area waiting for their chance to dock. The *Outrider,* being here on royal business, was able to skip the queue and proceed directly to the Rainecourt family's reserved tower.

Grayson wished that for his first time back, he would have been allowed some time to do a little sightseeing. Who knew when the next time his duties would take him to the capital? But he knew whatever he had been called here for was likely of the highest urgency. At least, it better be, or he would be quite upset at having been given less than an hour between when he was told he was being reassigned to the Sentinel Guard and having to be ready to depart on the ship.

A man in the crisp uniform of the Royal Sentinel Guard was waiting for him as he disembarked. He was an older guy with the weathered look of someone with a lifetime of service. "Captain Grayson. I'm Lieutenant Orbin. I'm to escort you to the Academy right away. They want you in the War Room."

"Not even time to change my coat," Grayson lamented. "Very well. Let's not keep them waiting."

They proceeded to a large, cog-shaped platform. The platform's attendant turned a dial a few times, then pulled a lever. There was a burst of steam from the edges of the platform and the outer rim started to spin. After a small amount of shaking, the platform slowly began to descend at a gradual angle.

A combination of steamwork engineering and Tether-bonding. Grayson knew that Rainecourt had long-standing treaties with the kray kingdom of Steinard in the Corbian mountains, masters of steam engineering, and the Komu Empire in the northlands, masters of steam Tether-bonding. This treaty allowed for the trade of their technology and equipment. The steam moved the gears along the tracks, while the Tether powered the steam. Put together, these platforms could take you quickly to any of the city's major circle districts.

Quickly being a relative term. Certainly faster than any other means of traveling the city, but it still took a while if one was going across the breadth of the city as they were.

"I'm a little disappointed Commander Marzin didn't come to greet me personally," Grayson said, just trying to make conversation to pass the time. "It's been a while since he last came out the boonies."

Orbin looked uncomfortable. "You haven't heard? The commander—he was killed in battle a few weeks ago."

That news hit Grayson like a sack of bricks. He didn't know Marzin too well personally, but he had looked up to him. The guy seemed indestructible and had unparalleled swordsmanship. Grayson had the honor of sparring with him a few times and getting to know just how big a gap there was between them. A gap he would never get to test how close he had come to closing.

"I can't believe that," Grayson said, stunned. "Who could have managed to bring down the Commander?"

"Pirates seized the *Lord of the Skies* while the Commander was on board," Orbin explained. "While we don't know exactly how things played out up there, we both know Marzin wasn't the type to give up the ship without a fight. Unfortunately, they sent his head back in a box."

Pirates? That was insane. If he had been told Marzin had been killed by a swarm of small dragons riding bigger dragons strapped with cannons, he might have believed it. But pirates? What a stupendously mundane way for a man of his skill to find his end.

"So, is that what this is all about?" Grayson asked. "Go find some pirates, get some revenge, recover the flagship? If so, I'm all on board for getting some justice for the commander."

"Possibly. I don't have the details of your assignment," Orbin admitted. "Though the king has already dispatched a fairly sizable force to go after the pirates."

"Well, if not that, what could it be?" Grayson wondered out loud.

"You'll find out shortly. We're here."

The military circle was packed with blocky, nondescript buildings. It was form over function as they needed to house thousands of soldiers and their families, store weaponry and equipment, and double as fallback shelters in case the city was ever invaded. The only structure that stood out was the Academy. It was a castle built in the old style, with two spires anchoring a grand wall which surrounded the main building. The only way in was through the heavy gate at the front.

It had once served as the military headquarters for the entire kingdom. Nowadays, every branch of the kingdom's military had its own center of operations, and the castle had been converted to an academy to train the most promising recruits to eventually join the Sentinel Guard, the royal family's protectors and elite special forces.

The only part of the castle that had remained unchanged from its original purpose was the War Room. Here, the king could directly meet with advisors from every branch of the military when the situation called for it. That was not lost on Grayson as he passed through the Academy and was led downstairs to the secure bunker which housed the War Room.

The layout of the room was simple: walls that were bare except for maps of the kingdom's major cities; a round stone table in the center with two dozen chairs surrounding it; and a board designed in the layout of the kingdom, covered in pieces that represented the current locations of the kingdom's military forces.

There was only one person already in the room when Grayson arrived, but he was a big one. The oni was eight feet tall, as bulky as two men put together, and had horns that would make any bull envious. The uniform he was wearing had been modified for his kind, but even then, it stretched and strained beneath his muscle. Grayson noticed several buttons were missing, probably having been discarded after just popping off from the pressure.

The giant approached Grayson. Grayson had seen and worked with oni during his time at Rainecourt's base in the Komu Empire as part of their treaty, but this one seemed to have an even more intimidating sense about him.

"Yulen SilverTalon," the oni said, extending a meaty hand towards Grayson. "Sentinel Guard Private."

Grayson extended his own hand and was grateful the oni didn't take the opportunity to squeeze his fingers into sausages. "Captain Grayson Lionsmane, formerly of the Komu Dispatchment Division, but presently assigned to Sentinel Guard."

"Lionsmane?" Yulen grunted. "You're General Urban's whelp?"

"The general is my father, yes." Grayson felt he knew where this was going. Many of his peers saw someone as young as him at the rank of captain and thought that his father had pulled strings to get him that position. It was quite tiring having to prove to everyone he met that he had earned his position through hard work and his specialized skillset.

Though it turned out, Grayson did *not* know where Yulen was going with this.

"He still owes me forty crowns," Yulen said.

"Excuse me?" Grayson asked, caught off guard.

"Forty crowns," Yulen repeated. "He made a bet with me last time I served under him that I couldn't kill more daemons on my own than the 12th battalion. I killed eight of the bastards and the 12th only took out seven. Urban said the eighth didn't count because it fell back down the Great Pit before it died, but I'd already crushed its body in! It was good as dead. As far as I'm concerned, that's a victory for me, and the general's got to pay up."

Grayson blinked in confusion. "I will be sure to bring it up to him next time I see him."

Yulen nodded and strode back to the table. He took a seat—well, two seats.

"Is it normal to have a private present for a meeting in the War Room?" Grayson asked Orbin.

"Don't let his rank fool you," Orbin answered. "Yulen's been in the guard longer than anyone else alive. An oni's lifespan is an impressive thing. In that time, he's turned down that many opportunities for advancement due to a desire to remain in the field. And there are few people with his experience surviving against incredible odds."

"So, if the king called him here, he's probably expecting this assignment to be pretty..."

"Deadly," Orbin confirmed. "But you can verify yourself."

As he spoke, the doors opened up and Davies Raincourt, King and Protector of Rainecourt, stepped inside. He was accompanied by the Foreign Affairs Minister, Astir Cotis, and a representative of the High Court, High Judge Indijo. The three men already present bowed properly to their sovereign.

"Please, dispense with the formalities for today," Davies declared. "I will make it an order if I must. There are things we must discuss that pertain not just to the future of our kingdom, but to me personally as a man and father. As such, I need our conversation to be frank and direct, and those present need to be able to speak openly if you believe my actions are being guided more by personal desire than the good of the kingdom as a whole."

That was a high ask for Grayson, who was already feeling well out of his league. He had never met the king before and had only seen him once from a distance when the king was addressing the force in Komu. The other two he only knew by reputation and their official portraits. They were among the most powerful people in the kingdom.

Yulen didn't seem to share the same nerves, as he quickly plopped back down in his seats after the king's declaration. "Is this going to be all of us?"

Davies nodded. "The smaller the group, the better. If any of this gets out, it could have dire ramifications."

"Why don't you start from the beginning, your majesty?" asked Minister Cotis, a middle-aged Kray with a bushy mustache and a stouter build than was typical of his people, though he was distinctively short.

The king took a seat at the head of the table, folded his hands in front of him, and began. "A few weeks ago, our flagship, *The Lord of the Skies,* was attacked and captured by pirates. Everyone on the crew was killed, as was the court's High Mage, Alarus, and the Commander of the Guard, Marzin. While it has been difficult to keep this from the public knowledge, the next bit is only known to a few: my daughter, Tara, was on that ship, returning from observing the Corbinite Trials."

Grayson's jaw dropped. "Was the princess slain?" He winced after he spoke, realizing he should have been more tactful when talking about a man's daughter.

"We do not believe so," Davies answered. "She was not among the dead the pirates discarded. We've been operating under the assumption that capturing Tara was the main objective of the pirate attack, and taking the flagship was incidental."

Yulen slammed a fist on the table, shaking the stone. "Tell me where the pirates are located! I'll go there, smash all their skulls, and bring back the princess personally."

While Grayson wasn't so dramatic, he agreed wholeheartedly with that plan.

"It is not quite that simple," the king explained. "We dispatched several sky divisions to pursue the pirates, but they've been led on a wild goose chase. The pirates show no desire for a fight, but they're also not flying across the border where pursuit would be more challenging. They seem to be intentionally wasting our time. We had trouble figuring out why they would be doing this, until I received a message that suggested that Tara was no longer in their possession."

"A message?" Grayson asked.

"A message sent via Tether," Davies expounded. "The sender was an amateur and their message was barely audible, but I was able to make out the words. They claimed that Tara had been taken to Bloodstone and was currently the captive of Clan Delmass. If that is true, then the pirates have been serving as a distraction all this time to keep us from looking elsewhere."

"Bloodstone," croaked the ancient Judge Indijo. He stroked his massive white beard. "That is a problem. We have no binding agreements with any of the necrid clan heads. There is no one we can pressure to demand Tara's return."

"The only option is force," agreed Minister Cotis. "Though with the necrids, that's not an easy proposition. A large-scale assault would be incredibly costly, in both money and lives. It would be hard to get the Council on board for such an action, even if it was in the name of saving the princess."

Grayson saw Yulen about to slam the table again and decided to beat him to punch.

"We're not just going to leave the princess there, right?" Grayson said, smacking the table, then regretting it as his hand was sore. "That's why you called us here, right? To go gut some necrids and get the princess back?"

The king nodded. "If we send any kind of large force, it is tantamount to a declaration of war. We'd be locked in a fight with all the clans of Bloodstone, one we might not be able to win. But a small team might be able to infiltrate the Delmass estate and extract Tara. This would be an incredibly dangerous mission. If you're exposed, you'd be stuck in a foreign land surrounded by necrids. If you're up to the task, I'd like you to lead that team, Captain Lionsmane."

"Of course I am," Grayson replied. "I'm not going to let a bunch of bloodsuckers rob us of our princess."

"I'm going to be on this team, of course," Yulen declared.

Davies nodded again. "You know the members of the Guard here well. Help the captain pick the rest of the team. And if things do go south on this mission, use your experience to help him guide the team home."

"My experience, my hammer, same difference," Yulen replied.

"This action won't be sanctioned by the Council," Minister Cotis reminded them. "If you get caught, it'll be as renegade actors without the kingdom's approval."

"Which means, even if they let you go, we might have to treat you as criminals on your return," Justice Indijo added.

Grayson was not deterred. "Then we'll just have to not get caught."

"Good." The king rose from his seat. "Any equipment or supplies you need, I'll see you receive. Once you're over the border, though, you're on your own."

"What about the person who sent the message?" Grayson inquired. "Might they be an ally?"

The king shook his head. "Unfortunately, I know nothing about them. The clans of Bloodstone are not unified. They are in a constant contest for power. It is possible the message was sent from one of Delmass' rivals in order to weaken them. Though there shouldn't be any mages among the necrids, so even that theory holds little water. I wouldn't rely on any help, anyway."

Yulen rose, knocking over both of his chairs in the process. "No point in sitting around here anymore, then. Come on, Captain! I'm ready to bust some necrid heads!"

"You do realize that, ideally, this is a stealth mission?" Grayson asked.

The oni laughed. "You know as well as I do how those always turn out."

He's not wrong, Grayson thought.

On the lowest circle of the city, in a neighborhood the guards did not often patrol, on a crowded street full of smoke shops and pleasure dealers, was a seedy bar called the *Dusted Glass*. It was not the kind of place you would expect to find a Sentinel Guard, particularly not one who could be relied on in a high-stakes mission. But this is where Yulen insisted they would find a "necessary member of the team."

Grayson looked around, trying to see if he could spot their recruit before Yulen pointed them out. Nobody looked promising among the drunkards at the bar. The tables were occupied by young men who looked like they'd never lifted a sword in their life. A few women going between the groups were selling a different kind of service than protection. He doubted any of the Guards would do that as a side gig.

Yulen pointed to a booth at the far end of the room, in a corner that was mostly covered in shadows. "There he is! Always likes to sit in a corner by himself. Won't even buy you a drink if you sit next to him. Hey, Jai!"

The man in the booth was a Kray, and like most of his kind, he was short and thin, though there was a certain rigidity to his build as well. If Kray were wiry by default, he was a wire that had been stretched taut. His eyes were sharp with suspicion. While he had one hand on his cup, the other remained close to the knife at his side.

Grayson knew this type. They rarely were the heroic sort.

"Hey, Jai!" Yulen repeated as he reached the booth. "Let me introduce you. This is Captain Grayson. And Captain, this is Jai Hazzen, specialist of the Sentinel Guard. We got a big mission, Jai!"

"Good for you," Jai replied, dryly. "I'm currently on my leave, so if you're trying to drag me into something, you can forget it. At least for the next week or so."

"Come on, Jai!" Yulen pleaded. "We need you on this one. It's all sneaky. You know I'm not good at the sneaky. What would the commander say if he was here?"

"The commander's dead," Jai replied. There was bitterness in his voice. "So, I guess it doesn't matter what he would have wanted now."

Grayson stepped up. "You really part of the Guard? You look more like the criminal type to me."

Jai scoffed. "You've got a good eye, then. But I hung up that mantle and took to this line of work a decade ago, so you're a little late."

"Well, you still got the selfishness of a criminal," Grayson countered. "You won't even hear what the mission is before you turn it down? You don't even want to hear what kind of stakes caused us to seek you out?"

With a sigh, Jai said, "Fine, tell me the details. But I'm going to keep drinking while you do."

Quiet enough not to be overheard over the din of the bar, Grayson gave Jai the rundown on what the current situation was and what they were up against.

"Well, fuck me running, you didn't pick just any mission to lead," Jai said once he had heard everything. "And you had to do this now? You couldn't let me enjoy the rest of my leave before going on a suicide mission to save the princess?"

"So, you're coming?" Grayson asked.

"One condition," Jai said. "I want you to bring Katura Simmore onto the team. She's a mage, and a pretty damn talented one."

"A mage would be a useful member of the team," Grayson agreed. "But what makes this Katura special?"

"I don't want to die, and she's pretty good at making people not dead," Jai replied. "Plus, having a life mage may come in handy when dealing with not-quite-dead necrids. Anyway, that's my condition. We have a deal?"

"Deal," Grayson agreed.

"I knew we could count on you, Jai!" Yulen joyfully exclaimed. "This will be just like old times."

Jai grimaced. "I sure hope not. Last time it took me a week to get all the blood washed off."

"It's not my fault! Who would have guessed those beasts would squirt so much blood just from breaking off their jaws!"

Grayson left the two of them to argue and went over to the bar. One drink for the road.

Based on what he'd seen so far of his team, he was going to need it.

Chapter 6

Three days and several flights by airship later, Grayson's team found themselves at the border of Bloodstone. If they squinted hard over the mountains, they could just make out the hazy sky that covered the city proper and obscured it from the sun. It was an ominous portent, although it may work in their favor. They intended to arrive in the early morning, before the city's residents arose, and the darkness would help conceal their movements.

The team waited on the shore of the Bloodflow River, waiting for a boat that was supposed to be piloted by one of Jai's contacts. There was no way they were going to be able to sneak an airship over the mountains and into the city, so they were going to be traveling the old-fashioned way. Grayson hadn't met this contact yet, but Jai had insisted they were reliable.

Hopefully more reliable than the mage he had insisted on bringing onto the team. As with every other day since the team set out, Katura had not shown up to the meeting place on time. Grayson didn't know if she was oversleeping or just didn't see the urgency of their mission.

"Should I send a message to Katura reminding her where we are?" asked Tomas, the fifth member of their crew. He was an air utility mage specialized in Tether-based communication. Though he wasn't an experienced combatant, by his own admission, Grayson knew from experience that the easiest way for a dangerous mission to go wrong was through a breakdown in communication, which was why he prioritized recruiting someone who could magically keep them in contact with one another. Each team member was given a ring that Tomas enchanted with a glyph spell, linking them together so they could communicate in the field.

Though he hadn't intended to use him as a babysitter. "We'll give her another minute," Grayson said. "Since the boat isn't here yet."

"She is a bit of a—what is the expression in your language? 'Odd duck?'" remarked Starc, the sixth and final member of the rescue team.

Jai side eyed Starc. "Look who's talking."

"Hey, I am no duck," Starc countered. "I am more of a raven, if anything."

Starc was an avian lyrian from the island of Kamura, as evidenced by his vestigial wings and pointed facial features. He struggled a bit with the native tongue, but he was apparently a master of the dual-sword style of his homeland, which earned him a lot of respect within the Guard. He'd come highly recommended when Grayson asked around about the best swords stationed in Aurelia's Hold.

"Ravens tend to have black feathers, don't they?" Jai said. "Yours are pretty grey. Or are you just getting old?"

"The rudeness, to insult a man's feathers to his face!" Starc exclaimed. "Do you have the trouble seeing colors? They are black as the night sky!"

Grayson was saved from any more argument when Katura finally showed up. The life mage did not seem dressed for combat, but instead was in a nice, breezy dress with flower patterns on it. She also had a bunch of earrings in different styles in both of her ears that jingled as she walked. Sentinel Guards were given some freedom on how they chose to dress on missions, but she was taking it to an extreme.

"You're late," Grayson said as Katura reached the rest of the group. "You have any idea what time it is?"

"Time is a slippery thing," Katura replied, seemingly unconcerned. "It is impossible to catch but easy to lose. It is best not to stress about that which we cannot control. Tell me, did I miss the boat?"

"No," Grayson admitted after a pause.

"Then all is well," Katura declared.

Sighing, Grayson decided to move on. "Is that what you intend to wear?"

Katura twirled, showing off her dress. "Do you like it? I think it brings out my eyes."

"You realize we are potentially going into combat?"

She looked thoughtful for a moment. "Do you think I should have gone with the sea patterns instead?"

Grayson could feel a headache coming on. He wondered if it was not too late to scrap this team entirely and start over.

The boat arrived, putting an end to that thought. It looked like a large fishing vessel that had been painted black and clumsily reinforced with sheets of steel.

The ship's captain stepped off. He was a seedy-looking man with one eye and hair that looked like it had never been washed. "Alright, Jai, you know the score. Money up front before anyone so much as steps foot on deck. And don't be trying to negotiate any discounts this time. Not where you got me sailing."

Jai gestured at Grayson. "This is Captain Grayson. He's the one holding the purse. Grayson, this is Terris."

Grayson examined the ship and its owner and quickly came to a conclusion. "You're a smuggler."

Terris snorted. "Yeah, what of it?"

"This is the contact you trust to bring us in and out of hostile territory?" Grayson asked Jai. "A common criminal?"

"I take offense to that, sir," Terris growled. "Ain't nothing common about me. I'm damn good at what I do."

Jai shrugged. "We are trying to smuggle out a person, aren't we? Who better to help us than a smuggler?"

It wasn't unreasonable logic. Grayson turned back to the smuggler. "You have experience sneaking across the Bloodstone border?"

"A bit. There are a few hidden docks I am familiar with, including one close to where you're wanting to be going. Though you might not like what you find there. I'll explain more when we get there."

It didn't look like they were going to have much of a choice but to trust this smuggler. Grayson wondered what his father would think about this.

"You'll get half of your payment now," Grayson declared. "And the other when we are safely returned. Something to keep you from choosing to abandon us once you drop us off."

Terris laughed. "Smart. I accept."

Grayson paid the smuggler, and moments later, the small team was sailing down the river, heading into the darkness on one of the most dangerous missions of their lives.

As the boat sailed into the bounds of Bloodstone's misty sky, Grayson felt a deep sense of unease. He'd known logically that the Bloodstone was eternally dark, but there was a difference between knowing something and experiencing it. It felt so unnatural, like he was traveling to a different world entirely where mortal men should not venture.

"We're almost there," Terris informed them. "Be getting yourselves ready."

"You mentioned something about not liking what we would find at these docks," Grayson reminded him.

"Aye. You familiar with 'ferals'? Necrids gone wrong. Well, more wrong. Their bodies are decaying while they still live, and the whole thing drives them mad. They become driven by naught more than their blood thirst. Some clans put them down. The Delmass, though, like to keep them around in case they need the fodder. The dock we're pulling up at? It's right next to their pen."

"So we're bound to get jumped by a bunch of mindless bloodsuckers the moment we step off," Grayson said. "That's not exactly ideal. Is there anywhere else you can take us?"

Terris fixed his one eye on Grayson. "Not if you want to be getting to where you're going this side of today. That's the only hidden dock in the Delmass territory. I can take you into the lands controlled by the other clans, but you'd have to find your way through that region, into the Delmass territory, then back out again. Personally, I'd rather take my chances with the ferals."

The longer they were here, the better their chance of getting discovered and having to fight real necrids. Terris was right, this was the best choice.

"What's the problem?" Yulen asked. "We go in, bash some feral heads, and go grab the"—he eyed Terris, trying to quickly correct himself—"the... prisoner. Easy."

"I wish I had your confidence," Jai remarked.

"The good news," Terris added, "is that if you can make your way up the path from the dock, your target will be close. There's a passage there that takes you right to the bottom floor of the Delmass estate. The cells your prisoner would be kept in would be right there."

Some good news, for once. If they could just survive the onslaught of the ferals, they might get out of here quickly without having to confront any true necrids.

"You're surprisingly knowledgeable," Grayson remarked.

"You don't make a living as a smuggler if you don't know the routes the goods pass through. But if anyone asks, I told you nothing."

They docked at an old pier, overgrown with weeds and swamp vegetation, which definitely qualified as hidden. Grayson made sure everyone knew what they were likely to expect and to have their weapons ready.

"You stay here with the ship," Grayson commanded Tomas. "I'm counting on you to keep us linked."

"You got it," Tomas said.

Quieter, Grayson added, "And if the smuggler starts to get squirrely and seems like he's going to take off without us, do what you have to do to stop him."

Tomas nodded his understanding.

Yulen led the way off the ship, hoisting his massive war hammer over his shoulder. Grayson followed and took a position to the oni's left, and Starc took the position to his right. Katura and Jai took the rear.

They proceeded up a narrow stone pathway that passed between two sheer, black walls. Water dripped down the walls from some unseen source, forming deep puddles along the path. Grayson winced as he stepped in one puddle that went up past his ankles. His socks were going to be soggy all day.

It was quiet for a while, with no sounds but the running water and their own footsteps. But ten minutes up the path, they began to hear shrieks. Loud, piercing, painful. They were followed by the sounds of frantic running.

They were coming. A lot of them.

"Positions!" Grayson commanded. "We push our way through these ferals. Don't buckle. This is for the princess!"

He received calls of affirmation as the first of the ferals appeared in front of them. They looked like corpses that had somehow pulled themselves from the grave. Their skin was rotting, their bodies were decrepit, and there was no humanity in their eyes. Grayson drew his weapons, a sword in one hand and a pistol in the other, and cleared his mind for the fight.

The firing of his pistol signaled the start of the battle. He picked his shots carefully, and his bullets found homes between the eyes of the approaching assailants. Body after body dropped, falling to the ground and tripping up the ferals behind them. They did not slow, though, showing no fear at the deaths of their companions. They climbed over one another, living and dead, desperate to satiate their hunger.

Yulen swung his hammer at the closest of the ferals as they reached the group. The creature's head exploded from the impact, sending shards of skull and brain matter in all directions.

Grayson didn't have long to reflect on the brutality of it before he was forced into melee himself. He swung his sword low, taking out the legs of his attackers and sending them to the floor. Finish them later, clear them now. One got too close for his blade, so he put a bullet into its chest. Another grabbed him from the side and tried to get its teeth into him. He shoved his pistol into its open mouth and gave it a meal it wasn't expecting.

There were dozens of them. For every one they killed, it seemed another two appeared at the end of the path. The pile of bodies swelled.

He was aware of Yulen swinging his massive hammer and swatting away the ferals like they were dolls. Of Starc cutting off limbs and slicing with the ease of a practiced butcher. Jai singling out targets that tried to get behind them and impaling them dozens of times with his knives.

Katura's earrings glowed as she brought her hands towards the attackers, and Grayson realized that they were her focus. He wasn't sure what she was casting, or what the sigil that appeared in front of her hands meant, but the ferals apparently were not fans as their bodies began to fall apart right in front of her.

Yet as many as they had killed, there were still more. It was only a matter of time before one of them slipped and wound up as a meal. They needed a way to quickly decide this battle.

Grayson had an idea.

"Fall back ten meters!" Grayson ordered. "Yulen, slow their advance for fifteen seconds, then bring 'em to me!"

"You got it!" Yulen replied.

As the group backed up on the path, Grayson flipped a switch on the side of his pistol. Sparks began to appear alongside the side of the gun and the glyph on the chamber began to glow. He was careful not to let his fingers slip from the rubber grip, lest he get shocked.

It was time to give these ferals a lesson in Rainecourt engineering.

Yulen smashed one last feral's head open before retreating to join the rest of them. One of the ferals grabbed him as he turned and sunk its claws into his side. He roared, grabbed the feral by the head, and smashed it against the wall.

Grayson watched carefully as Yulen led the attackers towards him. As they reached the big puddle and stepped into it. As Yulen's feet cleared to the other side. At that moment, Grayson fired.

A bolt of electricity hit the puddle and sparks began to fly. The water carried the electrical current through all the ferals inside of it. Their bodies twitched and spasmed as the electricity fried what remained of their flesh. More ferals joined them, heedless of the danger. Grayson fired another shot to keep the electric current from dissipating.

Soon, the group of ferals had been reduced to little more than charred husks.

"Damn, good thinking, Captain," Jai said. "Though I could do without the stench of burning flesh."

"Smells like victory to me," Yulen bragged. He started to laugh but doubled over, clutching the injury on his side.

"You're injured," Grayson said. "Do you need to go back to the ship?"

"This is nothing," Yulen insisted.

Katura went over to him and put a hand near his wound. "Stay still for a moment. I don't want any of that blood getting on my dress."

Her earrings once again lit up, and a bright white sigil appeared at her fingertips. Before their eyes, Yulen's wound began to rapidly close. Soon, all that was left was a deep scratch and dried blood.

"Gah, I always hate that!" Yulen shouted. "Feels like a bunch of spiders crawling under your skin and into your wound."

"Oh, don't be a baby," Katura responded. "I use that spell on children without them complaining. If you're good, I can give you a candy later."

"Hmm, I do like candy," Yulen replied, missing the implied insult.

Grayson flipped off the electric charge on his pistol. The glyph was good for six shots before it would need recharging. He had just expended two of them. Hopefully, he wouldn't need the rest, but the mission was not yet over.

"Catch your breath, and then get ready to move," he commanded. "Our job's not even half done."

A short while later, they found the passage that the smuggler had promised existed. Unfortunately, they found that it was not unguarded.

Three necrids were seated near the passage's entrance. From the look of their seats, their supplies, and their weapons, this was a regular outpost. Grayson wondered if Terris hadn't known about these guards or had just chosen not to warn them.

"Looks like they're more concerned with whoever is coming out of the passage than going in it," noted Jai. "We might be able to sneak up on them."

Jai was right. Their seats were positioned so they were all facing the passage. To watch for escaping prisoners, perhaps?

"Necrids have pretty good hearing," Grayson replied, remembering the briefing he had received on the opposition. "I'm not sure if approaching undetected is a possibility."

"It is for me," Jai insisted.

Yulen slapped Jai on the shoulder. "Jai is so brave. Volunteering to slay all three necrids."

Jai scowled. "I didn't say that. But I do think I can sink my blade into one of them before I'm noticed. Given how tough these bastards are supposed to be, that might give us the edge. Though it would leave me in the shit until you come back me up."

"I can cover you with my pistol," Grayson volunteered. "Though I'm not sure how many shots it takes to down a full-blooded necrid."

"I can clear the distance to them in ten seconds," Starc claimed. "I have a speed of an eagle in flight."

"You mean a raven?" Jai jibed.

"If we just need to keep them busy for a moment," Katura chimed in, "then I have an idea. I'm quite good at being distracting."

Taking the gamble on Katura and Jai's plans, the rest of the team waited out of sight while the two of them went ahead. Grayson switched on the electric shots of his pistol and kept it ready in case he needed to make a quick disabling shot.

Katura made no attempt at stealth. Instead, she walked straight up to the group of the necrids with as friendly an expression as if she were going to meet a group of friends.

The necrids were understandably surprised as they heard her coming. They got up from their seats and put hands on their weapons.

"Hold it, slave!" one of the necrids called out. "What are you doing out here?" He paused, seeming to think more about how strange this situation was. "*How* are you out here?"

"Hello, boys," Katura said, with uncanny casualness. "I think I may be a little lost. Can you help me out?"

"Have you lost leave of your senses?" the necrid growled. "You speak far too familiarly with your betters, girl."

Another of the necrids seemed more suspicious. "That dress—it does not seem like the kind of dress that would be given to a slave."

"Do you like it?" Katura twirled around, much as she had done to Grayson earlier in the day. "I wasn't sure if the colors would work in this low light, but I am pretty happy with the result."

"I don't know what game you think you're playing," the lead necrid said. "But it is apparent you need a fresh lesson in manners. And as a slave catcher, it is my pleasure to teach it to you. Wait right there."

The more suspicious necrid seemed like he was about to say something else. Perhaps warn his comrade that he sensed some danger. Unfortunately for him, he didn't get a chance.

Jai moved so silently that he might as well have been floating through the air. None of the necrids were aware of his existence as Katura kept their attention. Not until Jai got one of his knives around the suspicious necrid's neck and slit his throat—and also stabbed him a bunch of times in the spine with his other knife just for good measure.

The other two slave catchers were momentarily stunned by the sudden display of violence. Not for long, as they were quickly raising their weapons to deal with this threat, but long enough for Katura to cast her spell. Her earrings glowed and a dark sigil appeared in front of her. Lines of visible Tether extended from the sigil to the necrid.

The necrids did not like this. They doubled over in pain and let out inhuman howls.

"What have you—?" the lead necrid growled.

"Oh, don't mind me, love," Katura replied. "I just noticed you seem sick, so I'm taking the opportunity to break down all that nasty necroplasm inside of you. Don't worry—I don't charge for my healing."

The necrid took a painful step forward, raising his mace to strike at the source of his agony. Katura didn't move, nor so much as even flinch as the necrid powered through her spell towards her.

She slowed him down enough for Starc, who was almost as fast as he believed himself, to reach the scene. The slave catcher was surprised by the appearance of yet another enemy, and his movements were slowed by the influence of Katura's spell. Starc laid into him with a series of slashes. The necrid, proving the toughness of his people's reputation, refused to drop even after having been slashed a half dozen times. But his body was becoming a canvas of red. He didn't have long.

The last remaining necrid, realizing the seriousness of the ambush he had found himself victim of, turned to rush up the passageway. In a few steps, he got out of the range of Katura's spell. If he got beyond the bounds of the passage entrance, he would disappear from view.

They couldn't risk him getting away and warning the others. Grayson took his shot. The bolt of electricity burned into the back of the necrid's neck. The power arced through his body, causing him to spasm. He slammed against the wall as he lost control of his body. Still alive through his necrid toughness, but without control of his limbs.

Yulen reached him before he could recover, slamming his hammer into the slave catcher's head and pressing it further into the wall. By the time he removed his hammer, there was nothing left of the necrid's head but a mushy pulp.

Three shots down, Grayson noted as he switched off the electric charge of his pistol.

Starc's opponent finally fell under an onslaught of wounds too numerous for even a necrid's legendary healing. Katura released her spell and took a deep breath. Her spellcasting endurance was going to be another resource Grayson needed to keep a watch on. She had not been holding back since they got here, but eventually, channeling all that Tether would get to her. He knew mages relied on concentration and endurance to effectively cast.

"They weren't so tough," Starc said as he wiped the blood from his sword. "Like peacocks, all show."

"Just wait until we have to fight a group of them fairly," Jai warned. "You'll be tweeting a different tune."

"With any luck, it won't come to that," Grayson said. "According to the smuggler, the cells should be just through this passage. Stick close and be ready for anything."

Someone was making a racket down in the cells. Amaura had been on her way to clean the cells and check on Tara's condition again, but when she reached the top of the passage, she heard what sounded like several loud crashes.

Were the torturers doing something to Tara right now? No, it wasn't the right time for that. But what if someone else had decided to attack her? Worried, she quickly and quietly made her way down the passage.

Tara's cell had been broken open. A giant man—an oni, Amaura believed—stood triumphantly in front of the shattered door, holding up a massive hammer.

"Told you I could get it open!" the oni proudly exclaimed.

"And made a giant racket in the process," a kray man said. "If you had given me a moment, I could have picked the lock."

The oni shrugged. "Should have said something sooner."

There were five of them down there, surrounding Tara's cell. Human, kray, lyrian, oni. All heavily armed. Amaura crouched at the end of the passage and observed.

A young man in a yellow and black uniform stepped through the broken door and helped Tara to her feet. "Are you alright, princess? Can you stand?"

"I'll be okay, thank you," Tara assured him. "Thank you, sir—I don't think we've met."

"Captain Grayson Lionsmane, Royal Sentinel Guard. We've got a boat waiting to get you out of here. Stay close to me, your highness, and we'll get you home."

They're from Rainecourt, Amaura realized. She stepped out from her hiding place, not thinking carefully enough in her desire to bid farewell to her friend.

Grayson spun as he heard her. He drew a pistol in the blink of an eye and leveled it at her. Amaura realized that the other rescuers present also had their weapons ready.

Of course, I'm an Aborrent, Amaura thought. They probably can't tell the difference between me and a necrid. How foolish of me.

Just as she had resolved herself to take a bullet for her mistake, Tara stepped between her and Grayson.

"Stand down, Captain," Tara ordered. "She's a friend."

Grayson looked suspiciously between Tara and Amaura. He didn't lower his pistol, but he also didn't fire it.

"You—you got my message," Amaura managed to say.

"*Your* message?" Grayson asked, surprised.

"The one I sent to the king. I... I wasn't sure if the spell worked."

Tara's eyes widened in surprise, unaware her new friend had a connection to the tether.

Grayson looked confused, but he lowered the weapon. "Oh, it worked. Didn't expect that it was a necrid who sent it."

"Technically, I'm only half a necrid. An..." She hung her head in embarrassment. "An Aborrent." Looking up with her head still hung low, she expected the reactions of disgust she had grown accustomed to since her turning. To her surprise, none of them seemed to react, which for a moment made her feel normal.

Suddenly, the door to the passageway opened. Someone was coming. Tara's rescuers looked like they were ready for a fight.

"Hide for a second," Amaura said. "I'll get rid of them."

Grayson narrowed his eyes at her. The others didn't move, seemingly waiting for Grayson's command.

"We can trust her, captain," Tara said.

The captain nodded. "If you say so, princess. Let's conceal ourselves over in that corner. But keep your weapons ready in case she fails."

Amaura rushed back up the passage and found a group of three Delmass clan enforcers halfway down it.

"Freak, what is going on down here?" the closest of the enforcers asked her. "A loud crash was heard coming from down here."

"Sorry, that was me," Amaura lied. "I was assigned to change out the locks on some of the older cells. I had all the doors I removed stacked up together on a wall, but I guess I didn't balance them correctly and they all came crashing down. I apologize for my clumsiness."

The enforcer rolled his eyes, then slapped her hard across the face, enough to knock her to her knees. "Really? Can't even perform such a simple task without such a screw up? Aren't you good for anything?"

"I'm terribly sorry." She struggled to her feet and bowed deeply.

"You better be. You wasted our time. I'm going to make sure your little mistake is reported to the mistress. Do you understand?"

Amaura winced, and she wasn't acting. "Yes, I understand."

The enforcer waved her up. "Clean up your mess and finish your assignment. And try not to make any more racket. It's still early in the morning, and people are trying to sleep."

"Yes, I will. Thank you."

The enforcers left, satisfied with the story they had been fed. Amaura sighed in relief, then returned to the cells.

"They're gone," Amaura informed the team of rescuers.

"Thank you, Amaura," Tara said. "I owe you. And not just for that, or sending a message to my father. It was thanks to you I was able to maintain my resolve down here. If it hadn't been for your friendship, I might have broken long ago."

Amaura wasn't sure if she was still capable of blushing, but she felt like she was. "I'm just happy to be able to help. After all my screw-ups, it feels good to be able to do something right."

"You should come with us," Tara said. "Being a slave to these monsters is no way to spend the rest of your life. Come back to my homeland with me. I'll see you're taken care of. It is the least I can do after everything you've done for me."

"Princess!" Grayson exclaimed. "Is that really wise? I'll admit, she seems... helpful? But she's still a necrid. Even if we did bring her, the moment she's in the sunlight, she wouldn't be able to survive."

"Half-necrid," Tara reminded him. "I believe she can survive the sunlight. And if not, we'll find a way to shield her from it. It's better than leaving a friend behind."

It was tempting, but...

Amaura shook her head. "I can't. My family—both my parents and my sister—they were all taken to the processing centers. They were taken because of me, and my failure to become a full necrid. Every day, they're suffering. Locked in darkness while their blood is extracted for the necrids to consume. I don't deserve a kinder fate while they are still being tormented. The only thing that is fair is for me to remain here and take whatever fate deems."

Tara looked downcast. "I understand. Well, there's no other choice, then." She looked to Grayson. "Captain, I'm going to need you to rescue a few more people."

"Princess?"

"Tara?"

Their exclamations were simultaneous.

"I won't leave Amaura behind, and she won't leave her family behind. So, we have to go rescue them." Tara spoke matter-of-factly.

"That's—I can't ask you to do that," Amaura said. "It would be suicide."

"We have a chance to get out of here, now," Grayson added. "Every second we spend here, our chance of being discovered grows. And trying to go to these processing centers to rescue someone—it just isn't possible."

Tara was not backing down. "Tell me, captain. What is the creed of the Sentinel Guard? Is it cowardice in the face of evil? Is it to leave allies behind in enemy territory? Is it to leave innocent people to suffer horrible fates because rescuing them would be hard?"

Grayson looked down at his feet. "No. We always stand up to evil in its every form, we never leave a man behind, and we protect the innocent no matter the cost."

"So, you know what you have to do," Tara insisted.

The captain rubbed his eyes. "You spent far too much time with Commander Marzin, princess. He rubbed off on you way too much. Very well."

"You can't be serious," the Kray protested. "The mission wasn't suicidal enough for you already?"

The oni laughed. "Come on, Jai. If we left now, this would have been all too easy. Let's do some heroism worth bragging about."

Grayson put a hand on Tara's shoulder. "But I won't risk you doing this. We'll handle the rescue, but you'll wait at the boat. That's my condition, and it's not negotiable."

Tara nodded. "I'll leave the hero-ing to the heroes, then."

"Starc, take the princess back to the boat," Grayson ordered the lyrian with grey-feathered wings. "Have Tomas keep in contact with us. If this goes bad, have the boat take off without us. The princess's safety is the top priority."

The lyrian saluted. "On my flock's honor, I will protect her with my life."

Grayson turned to the rest of the group. "Jai, Katura, Yulen. You get to do the fun part with me. Ready for a stroll through Bloodstone?"

"No," Jai said.

"Yes," Yulen answered.

"I do enjoy strolls," Katura replied.

Amaura was stunned. "I can't believe this... you—you're really going to save my family?"

Grayson just shrugged.

"That's my job."

Chapter 7

Tara had nearly given up all hope of being rescued. As much as she had kept up a brave face in front of her captors and Amaura, she was only human. Her education in mastering the emotions shown on her face had come in handy, but if the rescue had taken much longer, she might not have been able to maintain the act. Even now, she struggled to believe the rescue was real and not just another dream.

As she saw the small craft that would take her out of this land of nightmares, the reality set in. In her fantasies, her rescue was always accompanied by some fanfare, and a magnificent airship lifted her to safety. The unimpressive boat that her rescuers had come in was far more in line with real life.

It was hard not to let her sense of urgency drive her to panic. A big part of her wanted to rush onto the boat and demand the captain depart immediately to get her quickly away from this place. But she needed to master herself and show some patience. She had promised Amaura a chance to rescue her family and had committed the majority of her rescue team to the effort besides. It was unthinkable to leave them behind.

"Watch your step, princess," Starc said, offering his hand to assist her stepping onto the boat. It seemed absurd, after everything she had been through, to be concerned with a slight stumble, but she took his hand gratefully anyway.

Another man was waiting on the boat. He sat cross legged on the deck, his eyes closed in concentration. Though Tara couldn't see the glyphs, she could feel the tingle of Tether being channeled around him.

"You still in touch with the captain, Tomas?" Starc asked.

"Indeed. I heard all about this seemingly misguided change in plans," the mage replied. "Grayson hasn't been caught yet, thankfully. We'll need to be ready to make a quick exit if that changes."

"The captain seems a competent sort," Tara replied. "We should have faith in him."

Tomas nodded. "As you say. Forgive me for not greeting you properly, princess, but I need to maintain focus on maintaining this connection."

Before Tara could reply, the door to the lower deck opened and a man with a shiftiness about him stepped out. He didn't look like a Sentinel. The ship's owner, Tara assumed.

"Did you manage to grab your prisoner?" the seedy man asked. "I don't want to be here any longer than I—"

He stopped midsentence when his eye fell on Tara.

"I might only got one eye, so my vision ain't quite what it once was, but I'm certain that's the princess of Rainecourt standing on my boat," the stranger declared. "And don't try and tell me it ain't. You never told me the prisoner we were rescuing was the bleeding princess! This was hardly the deal."

Starc took a step between Tara and the stranger. "Does it matter who we are rescuing, Terris? It doesn't change what you've been paid to do."

"Of course it matters!" Terris shouted, working himself into a fury. "And you knew it or you wouldn't have hidden it from me! Blast, it is one thing to take a prisoner from the necrids; it might make them a bit grouchy but not likely to make you mortal enemies. But if they went through the hassle of kidnapping the bleeding princess of Rainecourt and you come and take her back? That's the kind of thing that makes you a target."

Starc's hand drifted towards his sword. "You might want to lower your voice. We are still in enemy territory."

Tara realized if this continued, there could be a confrontation between the ship's captain and Starc. It was up to her to maintain the peace between her rescuers and the man whose boat they had commissioned.

She bowed down in front of the captain, a deep, respectful bow. This caught everyone on the ship off guard.

"Princess!" Starc exclaimed. "You shouldn't—it's not right for you to degrade yourself like that."

Tara ignored him. She had defended her family's pride every day since she had been captured, and it had taught her a valuable lesson on when it was important to maintain such dignity.

"Captain, you have the deepest gratitude of me and my family for your timely assistance in my rescue," Tara said, her tone humble. "You will forever be known as a hero in Rainecourt."

Terris fixed his gaze on her, but his expression softened a bit. "I ain't no hero, lass. I'm just a smuggler. A good smuggler, but not a heroic one. My missing eye is evidence of what happens when one steps outside the bounds of their station."

Tara did not raise from her bow. "A man is a complex thing. You are a smuggler, but you are also a hero to Rainecourt. You are not bound within a simple box. And however you view yourself, my gratitude is real."

"Fine, fine," Terris said with a sigh. "I get it, alright? I'm already deep enough in that it's not like I could do anything about it anyway. Just stop bowing. It's embarrassing. And where's the rest of the group?"

"They're going deeper into the city to rescue further prisoners," Starc replied.

Terris through up his hands in defeat. "Of course they are. Might as well break our agreement even more. I'm going to have a long discussion with Jai when this is all over."

When this is all over. Yes, this is almost over, Tara thought. Just a little longer and she could go home, and all of this would be like a bad dream.

She hoped Captain Grayson made haste.

Nobody paid much attention to Amaura's group as they made their way through the streets of Bloodstone. Those that did look their way paid more mind to Amaura herself, the Aborrent, than any of the inconsequential slaves with her.

The slave clothing Amaura had stolen from their quarters had been effective in disguising Rainecourt's rescue team. They weren't perfect fits, but slaves rarely had perfectly fitting clothes to start so it was nothing that would stand out. The only one not disguised was the one called Yulen. There was no one in the manor close enough to the oni's size. She instead gave him a large crate and instructed him to carry it behind the rest of the group. Make it look like he was just doing some physical labor. It was enough to help him blend in at first glance, though it wouldn't hold up to a second glance.

"The blood bank is just ahead," Amaura explained. "I know which building they are in, but not where inside. I also don't really have a good plan of what to do once we get inside. They're not just going to let a bunch of slaves start freeing the captives."

"I've got a few ideas," Grayson said. "Leave the hard part to us." He then looked up slightly, as if fixated on something in the distance. "Tomas, we're approaching the targets now. Be ready if things go sideways. Everything still peaceful there?" A pause. "Good. I'll keep you updated."

Communication through the Tether. Something far more intricate than what Amaura had done, and that allowed for the recipient to freely talk back. Amaura was fascinated by it, though it didn't seem an appropriate time to ask questions. She wondered if she could possibly do something similar.

They reached the exterior of the processing center where her family was being kept. Amaura felt herself freezing up as she faced it. Now that she had come this close, she had to face a terrifying possibility, one that she had buried in the deepest part of her subconscious, to be willfully ignored until it could be avoided no longer: What if it was already too late?

Her parents, she thought, were likely still hanging on. They had been taken as slaves when they were young and lived long lives surviving the harshest conditions the Delmass clan had to offer. They were as tough as old leather, more than strong enough to survive the conditions in the processing center. It was her sister she was truly worried about.

Tryphena had always been frail. Fragile. She never would have survived life as a slave if not for the special treatment Amaura's family received thanks to her falling in favor with the mistress. Tryphena was always put on light duty and was given more days to recuperate than any other slave serving Talia, in exchange for Amaura picking up the slack. She didn't have the constitution to survive something so terrible as blood extraction for long. Amaura didn't know what she would do if they broke into the cells only to find that her sister had long since succumbed.

"Steady, Amaura," Grayson said, apparently sensing her unease. "You'll need your wits about you. And we'll need your guidance."

Amaura forced her worries down and made herself focus on the task ahead of her. She had been given a chance at saving her family, a chance she never thought she'd have. However small the odds, she had to take it.

"I'm alright," she said. "But whatever plan you have, now may be the time to enact it. The moment we step inside, the attendants are going to want to know what we're up to."

Grayson nodded. "Alright, Yulen. Time for you to drop that crate. You're going to play a different role to help us get inside."

The oni dropped the crate unceremoniously to the ground. "I'm to be the cheese in this trap, eh? Not a fan. I prefer to be the mouse."

"The mouse is the one that gets caught in the trap!" Jai jibed.

"Not a clever mouse."

"Enough about mice," Grayson commanded. "Just follow my lead."

As they walked through the door, Grayson and Jai each held one of Yulen's arms behind his back, giving the impression they were escorting the massive oni as a prisoner. Amaura wasn't sure if even the two of them together could contain the big man if they really needed to, but the acting was believable enough.

They didn't get three steps inside before the attendant approached them. "Is there something I can help you with?"

The attendant was a bald necrid with a crooked nose and yellow teeth. He was accompanied by three others, large enforcers whose faces showed no sign of humor.

"Mistress Talia wants this oni processed for blood donation," Grayson answered.

"We didn't get any word to expect a new guest," the attendant inquired while looking over Yulen with interest.

"I know, but hopefully you got room," Grayson continued his lie. "This guy messed up real big today, and it was the last straw for the mistress."

Amaura bit her tongue. The story Grayson was telling was reasonable enough, but his speech, his expressions, and his tone were all very inappropriate for someone claiming to be a slave. She hoped he didn't give himself away.

Fortunately, the attendant seemed to be too fixated on the oni to notice. "I'm sure we can make room. You can just leave the troublemaker with us. I'll provide you with a receipt for Mistress Talia."

"Actually, the mistress wanted us to escort the oni to his room ourselves," Grayson added. "She was quite insistent about it, actually."

Amaura flinched. That was certainly one lie too far.

The attendant folded his arms. "Why would she do that? Nobody goes back there besides those that work here and the cattle. She knows this."

"The shortage of oni!" Amaura quickly chimed in, a memory of a different conversation held with the blood bank's manager coming to her in the nick of time. "I mean, the shortage of oni blood. It's become very expensive now, and she's been upset about how little she's been able to procure. This oni's blood is worth its weight in gold, and she wants to be certain there aren't any... complications."

"Are you accusing me of incompetence?" the attendant demanded, glaring at Amaura.

Amaura bowed. "I would never dare. I merely repeat the mistress's words."

The attendant looked away and grumbled. "The shortage of oni blood is from a lack of fresh cattle, not from any errors in the donation process. It is just like Talia to send her Aborrent pet to slap me in the face instead of talking to me herself. Fine. I'll let you observe the start of the donation process so you can report back that all is well. But don't touch anything while we're back there. There is a lot of sensitive equipment, and even a slight contaminant could ruin an entire batch of blood."

He nodded to his enforcers, then gestured to the door behind him. Two of the enforcers took positions near the front, standing guard while the attendant was away. The third accompanied them as they followed the attendant deeper into the center.

It was quiet back here, which was somehow more disturbing than the wails of misery Amaura expected. The victims here had given up to such an extent that they no longer even voiced their misery.

"We'll be taking him to the very back," the attendant said. "It is where we keep our VIP guests. Do you want my man to take over restraining the oni?"

"No, we've got a hold on him, thanks," Grayson replied.

The attendant glanced at him suspiciously. "I don't believe I've seen you before. I'm quite familiar with Talia's pet Aborrent, but the rest of you are unknown to me."

"We're—recent additions to the household," Grayson tried.

This only made the attendant more suspicious. "Is that so? How recent?"

Amaura chimed in to save Grayson. "They were just traded from the Panarin clan. The master there gave my mistress a good price because he was not pleased with how *talkative* they are."

"I can see that." The attendant smirked. "Well, a few months under the mistress's care should teach them proper manners. Or they may wind up as guests here themselves. Wouldn't that be fun?"

As they passed the cell doors that contained each of the center's victims, Amaura tried to stealthily peek through the small window slit in each, hoping to catch sight of her family. As they started to reach the end of the hall, she began to worry that she had missed them or had been misled on where they were being kept.

Then, through one of the final doors in the hall, she saw her—Tryphena. She looked awful. Her skin was pallid and sweaty. Her hair was clumped up around her ears and seemed to be falling out in places. But she was still alive. Amaura nearly leapt upon seeing her, only just remembering not to show any outward signs to the attendant. She did covertly signal the door to Grayson, who nodded.

In the next two cells, she saw her mother and father. They looked like they were holding up alright, all things considered. She wasn't too late.

Now they just needed pull off the rescue.

They reached the final door in the hall, which led to a cell twice as large as the others. The attendant took out a key and popped the door to the cell open.

"This is our oni suite," he declared. "It's got specially reinforced restraints to compensate for their strength, as well as considerations for their feeding tubes to ensure they remain healthy and producing blood for as long as possible. I'll show you our measures so you can report back to your mistress that her oni is in good hands."

"After you," Grayson said.

Amaura watched as the attendant walked into the cell, followed by Grayson quickly slamming the cell door shut behind him.

The enforcer was surprised and looked like he was about to attack Grayson, when Katura put her hands over his face. Glyphs formed across his temples.

"You've had a long shift, dear," Katura said. "Why don't you take a nap?"

The necrid wobbled on his feet and attempted to reach out and grab Katura, but his hands never came close to her. His eyes closed and he slumped back against the wall, snoozing.

"Well done, Katura," Grayson praised.

Katura wiped sweat from her forehead. "The big boy had a bit more vitality than I had expected. Between that trick and the power I expended earlier, I've nearly tapped my connection to the Tether."

"Save anything you got left in case one of us needs healing," Grayson ordered. "Now let's get these cells open."

Jai held up a set of keys. "You could have given me a bit of a heads up about what you were planning. I nearly didn't have the chance to pick these off of him."

Grayson scratched the back of his head. "I didn't even think about us needing the keys. Those are some quick hands, Jai."

"It's these three cells," Amaura told them.

Her father was released first. He was hooked up to a bunch of equipment that periodically drained his blood while forcing him to stay alive. Katura was able to unhook him from all of it, but he was left in a daze and didn't seem to understand what was going on. Even as Grayson escorted him out of his cell, he didn't regain his senses.

"Father?" Amaura tried. "Can you hear me? It's Amaura."

His response was a garbled mess.

"He's been through a lot," Katura said. "He needs proper care and rest. It may be a while before he comes around."

"Rest will have to come later," Grayson said. "Let's get the other two unhooked and get out of here."

Her mother came next. She was in a slightly better state. At least she was lucid, although just barely.

"Amaura?" her mother whispered. "What is—what is happening?"

"It's going to be alright, Mother," Amaura said gently. "We're going to get you out of here."

"The mistress," her mother continued. "She's letting us out?"

Amaura didn't know how her mother would react to hearing that she was being broken out by foreigners and was about to be taken away to a distant nation. She just held her mother's hand and nodded.

Finally came Tryphena. Amaura held her breath the entire time Katura was unhooking her from those disgusting devices. She was afraid the shock of being removed would be too much in her weak state.

Surprisingly, of the three, Tryphena seemed to regain the most strength once she was lifted to her feet.

"Amaura," she said, taking in her sister. "You look—different. I guess that must be the reason the mistress has been punishing us."

Amaura looked away, ashamed. "I'm sorry, Tryphena. It's all my fault. I failed to complete the Ascension and wound up an Aborrent, and you were all tortured as a result."

"It's not your fault. I know you've always done everything for us. You wouldn't have let this happen if you could control it. And look at you now, defying the mistress to break us out. I knew we could always count on you."

Tears welled up in Amaura's eyes as a mix of emotions battled within her. Relief that her sister was alright. Absolution for knowing she was not being blamed. And a new hope for the future that was unfamiliar. She rushed forward and embraced her sister in a hug. Despite the condition she was in, her sister hugged her back firmly. Perhaps she had underestimated Tryphena this whole time. She was a lot stronger than she had been given credit for.

"This is a very touching sisterly reunion," Jai called from the door. "But we're still deep in enemy territory and need to go before we're discovered."

"Oh, be quiet, Jai," Katura called back to him, wiping a tear from her own eye. "Do you have no heart?"

"Jai's heart is tiny because he is tiny," Yulen replied.

Tryphena looked over the group that had come to her rescue. "Your friends are strange, Amaura. I take it they are not from around here?"

Amaura nodded. "It's a long story, but they're going to get us far away from here."

"Anywhere is better than here. Let's go."

Tryphena was able to walk on her own after a bit of adjustment, though both of Amaura's parents required someone to carry them.

"I doubt there is any story we can tell them guards up front to explain why we're coming back minus the attendant, plus three prisoners, so be ready for a fight," Grayson ordered his men.

But it wasn't just the two enforcers from before who they found waiting for them. There were three more necrids there, wearing dark cloaks with hoods pulled over their heads. Mistress Talia's torturers. And leading the pack was none other than the chief torturer himself, Vents.

"So, this is what you've been up to, eh, Amaura?" Vents said, his tone as friendly as if this were a casual chat. "I thought it was suspicious when you refused my offer, so I decided to keep an eye on you. I never expected this kind of treason. Aiding foreign adversaries? Breaking into a processing center? Freeing prisoners? Not even someone as favored by the mistress as you will be coming out of this one with your skin intact."

Amaura was frozen in a combination of fear and anger. She knew there was no lying her way out of this one.

"A friend of yours?" Grayson asked. He and his companions had drawn their weapons and taken positions in front of Amaura's family.

"This is the chief torturer for the Delmass clan," Amaura explained. "He was the one charged with breaking Tara."

Grayson's expression was grave. "So this is the gentleman responsible for handling our princess so roughly. I'm glad I'll get a chance to personally thank him before we leave."

"Oh, you needn't worry about your princess, human scum. You'll be joining her shortly." The torturer laughed. "I already sent the slave catchers to bring her back. I'll ensure that you get a cell right next to hers so that you have front row seats to all the terrible things I'm going to do to her."

That taunt proved to be too much for Grayson, who responded by firing his pistol at the torturer. Vents moved with inhuman speed out of the way of the bullet and lunged forward.

Everything devolved into chaos after that as the torturers and enforcers engaged against Rainecourt's rescue team. It all happened so fast Amaura struggled to keep up with it. Grayson was firing off shots with his pistol. Yulen, whose hammer had been left outside in the crate, was wrestling with one of the enforcers hand-to-hand. Jai ducked between the legs of one of the torturers, slashing with his dagger as he went. Katura backed away from the fray, hands raised, looking for the best opportunity to use the rest of her magic.

The rescuers fought valiantly, but it was quickly becoming clear that they were outmatched here. The necrids were too strong. Too fast. They were getting pushed back, and soon they would be pushed into a wall, surrounded, and overwhelmed. Amaura tried to get over to where her family members had gathered, hoping to find some way to pull them out of this mess. Or, at the very least, be with them at the end.

She was grabbed before she could reach them.

"You made a big mistake when you decided to cross me, Aborrent," Vents whispered in her ear. "I know how to hurt people in ways far worse than merely killing them. For your treason against the Delmass clan, I'm going to show you true pain."

Amaura flinched, expecting to feel the sharp pain of a cut against her back. But instead, Vents let her go.

And leapt towards her defenseless family.

Amaura could only watch helplessly as her father was cut down, never to come back to his senses. Her mother was next. She looked down, resigned to her fate, before the blade struck her. Vents raised his blade next to her sister.

Grayson leapt into the way, pushing Tryphena to the ground. The attack scraped across his back, leaving a streak of red across his slave garbs and his uniform underneath.

Vents scoffed and kicked Grayson off of his target. Grayson rolled onto his back, aiming his pistol up as he did, and fired.

Sparks burst from the pistol. Vents tried to dodge out of the way, but his shoulder got caught in the electric blast. He growled in frustration as the lightning spread across his body, locking his muscles in place.

Amaura rushed over to her parents, but it was too late to do anything for them. She had just gotten them back, and they had already been taken from her. Taken to punish *her*. Taken because it was the cruelest thing that could be done to her. As if everything else that had been done to her wasn't enough.

At that moment, something snapped inside Amaura. All the hatred she had for Bloodstone, all the despair she had been put through, all the trials she had been forced to endure as a slave. Everything she had suppressed to try and do what was best for her family. It ignited all at once. She felt like her body was on fire.

Vents pushed through the electric paralysis to raise his blade. Tryphena was helpless below him.

The power that had been within Amaura all her life surged as the fire burned in her core. She held a hand out towards Vents. She wasn't even sure what she was doing. It was unlike anything she had done with this power before. All she knew was that she was pissed, and this power needed to be expelled.

A blazing glyph appeared before her. The symbols seemed born from flame, the natural path a fire takes as it consumes all before it. The fire spread, then exploded forth.

Vents barely had the time to look her way and realize what was happening before his body was completely engulfed in white-hot fire.

Everyone else stopped fighting to witness the scorching inferno that had appeared in the middle of them. They all stood there, as if watching a peaceful bonfire and not the conflagration of a man. The fire ran its course, leaving Vents little more than a charred corpse.

As the fire dimmed, the fighters regained their senses. Realizing what Amaura had just done, the necrids rushed at her. But she had yet more fury within her. Fireball after fireball flew from her hands, igniting a torturer, then an enforcer, and then the other torturer. The last of the enforcers reached her and grabbed her by the front of her shirt.

Only to be pulled off by Yulen, who then headbutted the necrid in the face before bull rushing him right through the front doors of the center and out into the morning gloom.

Katura rushed over to Grayson and laid hands on him to close the wound on his back.

"I'm sorry, Amaura," Grayson said. "I was too slow to save your parents."

A part of Amaura wanted to tell him that it was okay, that it wasn't his fault, that she was grateful that he had taken a hit to save her sister. But that rage was still burning within her, and she was afraid if she opened her mouth at all, fire would spit out of it, even if it was completely unfair to the captain.

Grayson picked himself off the ground and looked out into the distance. "Tomas, we're on our way out now, but you've likely got company on its way. Necrid slavecatchers. If you can't hold them off, get out of here."

"We got problems out here, too, captain!" Yulen called from outside.

Amaura helped her sister to her feet and then followed the rest outside. Yulen stood at the base of the processing center, holding the hammer he had recovered from the crate. Around him, a crowd was forming. Necrids and slaves, including enforcers, taskmasters, slavecatchers, and all matter of lower management. All gathered to investigate the ruckus they had caused in the processing center. They formed a tight semi-circle around the center, preventing any escape.

"Entire blasted city has come out to say hello," Jai said. "So much for a stealth mission."

"Plans, Captain?" Yulen asked.

"Honestly, I got nothing," Grayson admitted.

The entire city had come out. The city that Amaura hated. The people that she hated. The necrids who viewed themselves as her superiors. Her fellow slaves whose jealousy and competitive natures caused them to drag each other down. And that damn sky which never let her see the sun.

She called forth the fire once more, but not at any one person. Her hand was raised at the sky. She put every bit of her hatred, every last ember of that fire that burned with her, and brought it forward. The flames of her very soul erupted forth and scorched the sky.

The haze retreated from the flames. As the fire spread across the sky, the perpetual shroud shrank away.

And the morning light burst through.

For the first time in centuries, the sun warmed the land of Bloodstone. The gathered necrids shrieked and ran for cover as their skin sizzled in the daylight. They cowered in the shadows of the buildings, they ran inside, they raced to outrun the shrinking haze. Some weren't fast enough and collapsed, grabbing at their exposed skin in pain.

The slaves ran, too, more out of confusion and fear than anything else. Many had never seen the sunlight before, and though their skin would not burn, they didn't know how to react to this sudden change.

Amaura basked in the light she had brought to the city. It hurt her eyes, and her half-necrid skin slightly tingled unpleasantly as the rays beat down on her. But despite that, it was... beautiful. Pure. With her anger spent and the light upon her, she felt a sense of peace she had never had before.

And then she collapsed. There was no anger, no fire, no power left within her. She was empty.

Grayson picked her up and cradled her in his arms. "That was the most impressive use of the Tether that I've ever seen in my life. You sure are a mysterious one, Amaura. Thank you for opening the path for us. I'll take it from here."

With that, Amaura allowed herself to drift into unconsciousness, comfortable in the hands of the Rainecourt captain.

Moments after Grayson's warning had come in, Tara spotted the necrids rushing down the path towards the ship. The slavecatchers had come to take her back.

"There's quite a lot of them," Starc said. "We need to make a choice—try to hold out until the captain arrives, or escape with our feathers intact."

"We can't abandon the others," Tara commanded. "We have to wait for them."

"As you command, princess," Starc replied. "Though I would feel a bit better about it if I wasn't the only one on this ship who could fight."

"If you give me a weapon, I would be happy to fight by your side," Tara replied.

Starc arched an eyebrow in surprise, then tossed one of his swords to Tara. "If the captain asks, I protested vehemently."

The necrids approached. Tara and Starc prepared to defend the boarding plank with their lives. They were surprised when Terris came on deck.

He held a massive rifle over his shoulder, one that was longer than he was and nearly as thick. Terris grunted with effort as he lowered the rifle. The whole boat pitched slightly as the rifle came to rest on the railing.

"This thing ain't exactly legal where we come from," he said as he lined up his shot. "I hope you can keep this between us."

And he fired. The shot was booming and left Tara's ears ringing. The head of one of the necrids popped like a balloon. The rest of them stopped, startled and somewhat less confident than they were before. That hesitation cost them as one of their bodies was split open by another massive shot.

The necrids resumed their rush, more hurried and desperate than before. Terris fired again, and again, each shot turning a necrid into a meat balloon. It was honestly terrifying, and Tara couldn't help but wonder at the power of that weapon.

"Is that an airship turret?" Tara asked as the realization struck her.

"The core of it is," the smuggler admitted. "But with a few... less than reputable modifications, you get a rifle. An unwieldly one, but it packs a punch."

Tara was eager to learn more about these "modifications," but also realized it might not be a good idea to press the smuggler on such illegal activities. Besides, there was a more pressing issue. Though Terris had dropped half a dozen of the necrids, just as many were still coming and were just a few strides away from the ship.

Suddenly, the sky burst into flames. The dark haze that covered the city was scorched away, leaving the morning sun to shine through. The necrids *did not* like that. They abandoned all efforts of getting onto the ship, instead jumping into the water on either side to get away from the sun.

"What is that?" Tara asked, looking up at the flames that continued to move across the sky.

"A gift from your friend Amaura, apparently," Tomas said. He opened his eyes and rose. "I got word from Grayson that they will be here momentarily. Mr. Terris, please be ready to take off."

Terris sighed with relief as he let the heavy weapon drop. "Yeah, you don't need to tell me twice."

Amaura did that? Tara wondered, pondering just what manner of person she had befriended.

True to his word, Grayson and his team arrived moments later, carrying the unconscious Amaura. They brought with them Amaura's sister, though unfortunately it seemed that her parents hadn't made it. Tara would have to be there for her friend to help her grieve.

The second Grayson stepped aboard, Terris had the boat moving. Tension remained in the air until they were well clear of the dock and on their way to deep waters beyond Bloodstone.

Tara took one last look back at the city that had held her prisoner. Already the haze was returning to the sky as the massive pillars worked to replace what Amaura had burned. Even when the sun shined on the darkness of this land, it was but a brief, fading light.

But Tara had come away from the experience with one bit of bright glimmer. She looked at the sleeping Amaura and smiled.

If one shred of joy could be salvaged from that pit of despair , perhaps it had all been worth it.

Chapter 8

Grayson tried in vain to rub the sleepiness out of his eyes. In the two weeks since he had returned with Tara, he had been subjected to three different medal ceremonies, four feasts, two all-night parties, and more nights on the town than he cared to count. Surviving the rewards from his mission was proving to be almost as great a challenge as the mission itself. If they really wanted to reward him, they would let him rest.

He thought he was coming to the end of it, but then he was suddenly summoned by the princess herself for a meeting. When the princess asks for you, you put your need for sleep aside.

The Sentinels on duty showed him into the princess's study and shut the door behind them. Tara was waiting for him, seated on a plush couch. Bookshelves lined the wall behind her, filled with books on every topic from history to the Tether to swordplay. The opposite wall was filled with all matter of knickknacks that Grayson couldn't find a common theme for. A fire burned in its hearth and gave the room a pleasant warmth.

Grayson kneeled respectfully. "Princess. You wished to see me?"

"Please, Grayson, there's no need for such formalities," she replied. "Not after everything we went through."

He did not rise. "There is a level of decorum that needs to be maintained, princess. I know I get—less than proper when I'm on a mission, but at least here in the capital, I should strive for proper conduct."

Tara sighed. "I can make it an order, you know. But I'd really prefer if you lightened up on your own."

Since she insisted, and no one else was around, Grayson stood up. "As you say, princess."

"Tara."

"Huh?"

"My name is Tara, not princess."

"Yes, Tara."

"Good."

Thanks to the ministrations of both doctors and magic, Tara looked to be largely recovered from her ordeal. At least physically, though Grayson knew the unseen injuries of such an ordeal took a lot longer to heal. If they ever healed at all.

Looking at her now, cleaned up and no longer covered in bruises, he was struck by how stunning she was. Her eyes were radiant. Her lips were full and plump. Her body was... well, he really shouldn't be thinking about the princess's body.

"Something on your mind, Grayson?" Tara asked. "You seem to looking this way most intently."

Grayson cursed himself for being so stupid as to stare at the princess openly like that. "I was just reflecting, is all," he lied. "Seeing you here reminds me of just what we all went through in Bloodstone."

She nodded, hopefully believing his story. "It is an experience that will never leave me. And I am much changed by it. I have seen the naïvety of how I used to view the world . I used to think, as long as we believed ourselves to be at peace, it was alright to let down our guards a little. I now recognize that for peace to be maintained, there needs to be people who are ready to fight to maintain it at a moment's notice. That's where people like you come in."

"I just do my duty to the kingdom. Nothing more."

"You vastly underestimate yourself," Tara countered. "And I'm sure Amaura would agree. You saved her sister, at great risk to yourself. That was well beyond the bounds of your duty."

Grayson couldn't argue with that. "How is Amaura? I haven't seen her since we returned."

"She's having a tough time adapting to her new environment. Not surprising, given the conditions she grew up in. I'm doing everything I can to ease her transition, but unfortunately duty pulls me away far too often. I'm intending to write a recommendation for her to attend the Academy of Magical Arts. Given what she was capable of with no training, I imagine she will find herself quite a prodigy among those students."

"It can be helpful to a person who is lost to be given a sense of purpose," agreed Grayson, speaking from experience. "I should probably visit and check up on her."

"I'm sure she would like that. But I didn't just call you here to discuss Amaura. I want to talk to you about what your plans are moving forward."

Grayson scratched the back of his head. "Honestly, I'm not really too sure. I was kind of expecting that once this all was settled, I'd be dispatched back to our base in the Komu Empire. I wasn't sure whether this post with the Sentinel Guard would be permanent or not."

Tara leaned forward, suddenly eager. "Would you like it to be?"

"I guess it depends on what the duty would entail," Grayson admitted. "I'm not much of a 'sit on my hands' kind of guy. If being in the Guard means standing in front of the palace all day shooing away unwanted visitors and overzealous tourists, I'd probably be pretty miserable."

"I understand. You're a man of action. Which is exactly why I want to offer you a position leading a special task force within the Guard that serves directly under me and handles the kind of work that only someone like you can accomplish."

"A task force?" Grayson mulled it over. "Do you have the rest of the team already in mind?"

"Actually, I'm kind of hoping we'll be able to keep the rescue team together. Your group—while odd in a way—accomplished a very difficult and dangerous mission. I'd like to see what more you could accomplish as a team."

The thought of continuing to work with the airheaded Katura and the constant bickering between Jai and Yulen was enough to give Grayson a headache. Still, he had to admit, the team had functioned well.

"And what kind of work would this task force be undertaking?" he inquired. "I can't imagine the king's men or the great generals are going to want us stepping on their toes."

Tara face became serious. "I have a feeling things are going to get dangerous enough in the near future that it won't matter. I'll admit, some of my motivation lies with going after the pirate who murdered the commander and sold me to Bloodstone. But these acts are likely just the opening salvo in dangerous times that lie ahead. We must be prepared for further action by the Delmass clan, as well as anyone who has been supplying and aiding these pirates. I just can't shake the feeling there is something larger at play here."

Grayson could have lived the rest of his life without getting involved with Bloodstone again and been a happy man. Alas, it seemed like fate would eventually put him in the path of the necrids once more.

"When you put it like that, how can I refuse?" Grayson asked. "I'd be honored to lead your task force, princess."

"Tara."

"That's going to take some getting used to."

"Well, you'll have plenty of time." Tara smiled brightly at him. "We're going to be working very closely together from now on."

Grayson couldn't help but smile back.

Amaura wandered aimlessly through the bustling streets of Aurelia's Hold, her heart thudding in her chest, each breath a reminder that she was far from the life she had once known. The city was an overwhelming labyrinth of towering structures and winding roads, and despite having been in Rainecourt's capital for nearly a week, she still couldn't find her way around without getting hopelessly lost. Her eyes flitted toward the rotating platforms that whirled citizens up and down the city's levels. She stepped onto one hesitantly, clutching the rail as steam hissed from its gears, propelling her upward to what she hoped was the right street.

The clattering of the platform finally stopped, and Amaura stepped off into another crowded thoroughfare, where vendors shouted over one another, selling everything from brightly colored fabrics to fragrant spices. She moved through the crowd, her pale skin and stark white hair drawing furtive glances from passersby. Whispers followed her, the word "necrid" uttered as though she were a ghost wandering through their world. It seemed here they had no concept of an Aborrent.

Amaura pulled her shawl tighter around her shoulders, hoping to shield herself from their scrutiny. Her hand shook as she approached a small shop with a wooden sign hanging from a rusty chain. The scent of baked bread wafted out, tempting her. She hadn't eaten since dawn, and the day was already slipping into evening.

"Excuse me," she said softly to the shopkeeper, a stocky man with a greying beard. His eyes flickered up to meet hers before darting away.

He didn't speak but gestured at the display of bread loaves in front of him. Amaura hesitated, her fingers brushing against a coin in her pocket. She had been given a small allowance from Tara, but she didn't know if it was enough.

"Do you have... smaller ones?" she asked, her voice barely above a whisper.

The shopkeeper's brow furrowed. He glanced around nervously, perhaps unsure of how to deal with her. Amaura couldn't tell if it was her appearance or the uncertainty of her accent that made him wary. After a long moment, he reached under the counter and pulled out a smaller loaf, placing it in front of her.

"This is fine," she said quickly, handing him the coin.

He nodded, still silent, and wrapped the bread before handing it over. His eyes never met hers again. Amaura muttered her thanks and hurried away, her heart heavy. She had no idea whether the man had been rude or merely cautious, but it didn't matter. It was the same everywhere she went. She didn't belong here.

By the time she returned to the room Tara had given her, the sky had darkened, and the air carried a chill. Amaura sighed in relief as she closed the door behind her. The small, cozy room was a stark contrast to the overwhelming city outside. A single bed lay against the far wall, and the crackling of the small fire in the hearth was the only sound pushing back against the silence .

Tryphena was seated on the bed, her expression drawn tight as she stared into the flames. Amaura offered her a weak smile as she placed the bread on the table.

"I got us something to eat," she said, hoping to lighten the mood.

Tryphena looked up, her face softening only slightly. "Thank you." She took the bread without further comment, breaking it in half and offering one piece to Amaura.

They ate in silence for a few moments before Tryphena finally spoke. "How long do you think we can keep living like this?"

Amaura blinked at her. "What do you mean?"

Tryphena sighed, her gaze distant. "We're outsiders here, Amaura. Look at the way they treat us. You think it'll get better? Just because the princess helped us once doesn't mean she can solve all our problems."

"She will," Amaura insisted, though her voice trembled with uncertainty. "Tara said she's doing everything she can. She... she saved us, Tryphena. We owe her everything. Once she's less busy, she'll find more ways to help."

Tryphena's frown deepened. "She's a princess, Amaura. She has a kingdom to worry about. We can't depend on her like that. We're not her priority, no matter how kind she is."

Amaura's chest tightened. Tryphena had always been the optimistic one, the hopeful one, but now her words were lined with a bitterness Amaura had never heard before.

"You sound... so different," Amaura whispered. "This isn't like you."

Tryphena looked down at her hands, her voice barely audible. "Maybe I've just finally seen the world for what it is."

Amaura reached for her sister's hand, squeezing it gently. "Things will get better. I know it's hard, but we have to trust that Tara will come through for us. She already has."

Tryphena gave her a long, weary look before nodding, though her eyes didn't reflect the hope Amaura wished they would. "Maybe. But don't wait forever, Amaura. We have to learn to survive on our own."

Amaura didn't respond. She watched her sister return to staring into the fire, the flames casting long shadows across her face. Despite the warmth of the room, Amaura felt a chill settle deep in her bones.

Tara stood before the stone memorial, her heart pounding in her chest as she gazed at the intricately carved figure of Commander Galvin Marzin. His likeness was cast in an eternal pose of valor, sword raised, eyes locked on some unseen enemy. But no statue could capture the gravity of the man—the steadiness of his presence, the strength in his voice when he spoke of duty and honor. Nor could it encapsulate the horror of his final moments, when Darrian Blake had stood over his fallen form, blade glinting with malice, and severed his head without a second thought.

The memory rose like bile in her throat. Tara clenched her fists, her nails digging into her palms. She took a shaky breath, the air crisp and cold in the quiet garden of the royal crypt. The city was far behind them now, its noise and chaos muted by the high stone walls. Here, in this sacred place, it was just her, her family, and the memory of the commander who had given his life for hers.

"I'm so sorry," she whispered, staring at the stone. "You deserved more. You deserved better than to be betrayed by someone you trusted."

She knelt before the memorial, her eyes stinging with unshed tears. "You always told me that leadership comes with sacrifice. That we do what we must for the greater good, no matter how much it hurts. But I never imagined you would be the one to pay the price."

Her voice faltered. "I swear to you, Commander, we'll bring them to justice. Blake, the pirates, all of them. One day, they'll answer for what they did. I'll make sure of it."

Behind her, King Davies cleared his throat softly. "Tara."

She didn't turn. She didn't have to. She could feel her father's presence, steady and unyielding, as he always was. He had been her rock through all of this, a calm voice in the storm. But right now, his words felt like water dripping ineffectually over stone.

"Tara," he repeated, his tone more insistent. "I understand your anger. Believe me, I do. But justice and vengeance are not the same thing."

"I know," she replied, her voice strained. "But they took him from us. He didn't deserve to die like that."

"No," Davies agreed. "He didn't. But neither would he want you to lose yourself in pursuit of revenge. What happens when you catch them, Tara? What happens when the fire in your heart is no longer fueled by hatred? You can't let it consume you."

Tara closed her eyes, her father's words a weight on her shoulders. "I don't want revenge. I just want—" She hesitated. What *did* she want? "I want justice. For him. For all of us."

"Justice," her younger brother, Taron, scoffed from behind them. "That's not what you want. What you really want is to see Blake's head on a pike. Same way he did to Marzin."

Tara whipped around, her temper flaring. "Taron, this isn't the time."

"It's *exactly* the time," he shot back, stepping forward with that infuriating grin of his. The one that never failed to boil her insides. "You talk about justice, but we both know you're aching for more than that. You want blood. Admit it. Blake humiliated you, killed Marzin right in front of you, and now you're thinking about how good it'll feel to do the same to him."

Tara's jaw clenched. "You don't know what you're talking about."

"Don't I?" Taron folded his arms, his tone mocking. "All that training, all that duty to the crown, and you still can't admit what's really burning inside you. If you don't act now, someone else will take Blake's side. Do you really want to wait around for the next tragedy? Or are you going to stop playing nice and do something about it?"

"Taron," their father warned, his voice dangerously low.

But Taron didn't stop. "You've seen what happens when you hesitate, sister. Marzin's dead because you didn't strike first. How many more lives are you going to lose waiting for this so-called 'justice'?"

The sting of his words hit her hard, as intended. She rose to her feet, her fists still clenched. "This isn't about striking first. It's about doing what's right."

"Doing what's *right* won't bring him back," Taron sneered. "But it'll sure make you feel better, won't it?"

Tara's chest heaved with barely controlled fury. She turned away from her brother, her hands shaking at her sides. "I won't stoop to Blake's level. I refuse."

Taron snorted. "That's your problem. You're too soft. You'll never be able to rule if you're always trying to be the better person."

"Taron, that's enough," King Davies commanded, his voice cutting through the tension.

Taron shrugged, stepping back, though his smirk remained. "Suit yourself. Just don't come crying to me when more good men die because you couldn't act."

Silence fell between them, thick and oppressive. Tara stared back at the memorial, her resolve wavering. Taron's words echoed in her mind, mingling with the memories of Marzin's final moments, the way his body crumpled to the ground, lifeless. Her stomach twisted in knots.

Davies approached, resting a hand on her shoulder. "Don't let your brother's words poison your mind, Tara. Marzin believed in you. He saw a future in your leadership, one built on wisdom and strength, not impulsive actions."

Tara swallowed hard, nodding, though doubt still gnawed at the edges of her thoughts. "I know, Father. I just... I don't know if I'm strong enough to do this the way he would have wanted."

Davies squeezed her shoulder gently. "You are. And you'll find that strength when the time comes. But for now, grieve him. Honor him with the actions you take, not with bloodshed."

Tara's gaze drifted back to the stone figure, her heart heavy. "I'll try."

Davies smiled softly, though sadness lingered in his eyes. "That's all anyone can ask of you."

As they turned to leave, Tara cast one last glance at the memorial, her mind a whirlwind of emotions. She wanted to be the leader Marzin had seen in her, but how could she when the weight of vengeance pressed so hard against her heart?

Chapter 9

The first weeks at the Academy of Magical Arts were a whirlwind for Amaura. Every corner of the grand, sprawling institution seemed to exude magical energy—shimmering orbs of light radiated from their glyph-etched sconces in the corridors, glyphs glowed on the bookshelves helping students find tomes in the vast library, and students of every shape and size practiced spells in the open courtyards. Yet, despite the wonders that surrounded her, Amaura felt more like a shadow slipping through the halls, unseen except when someone cast her a wary glance.

Her first day in Professor Saelis' class had been marked by the usual whispers. She had felt their eyes on her the moment she entered the room, her pale skin and white hair marking her as an outsider. *Necrid, Aborrent.* The words hovered like a storm cloud over her wherever she went. She had tried to ignore it, keeping her head low and taking her seat at the far end of the lecture hall, but the murmurs followed her.

"They say she's a prodigy..."

"Or just a mistake."

"Princess Tara vouched for her, but why?"

Even her teachers hadn't been sure what to make of her. Professor Saelis, a stern man with a hawk-like gaze, had looked her over with thinly veiled skepticism during their first practical lesson. It wasn't until she had conjured a shield of pure Tether energy, pulsing with such strength that it vibrated through the entire classroom, that he had finally spoken.

"Impressive," he had said, rubbing his chin thoughtfully. "When the princess wrote of your potential, I'll admit I thought she was exaggerating. But perhaps she was not."

Saelis hadn't been the only one to doubt her. Master Kandor, an elder mage with flowing silver hair and a quiet demeanor, had openly questioned whether the stories of the firestorm she had summoned over Bloodstone were real or mere embellishment. "The sheer magnitude of such power is rare, especially in someone so untrained," he had said during their first one-on-one session.

But as the weeks passed, Amaura had proven herself time and again. She had a natural connection to the Tether that surpassed her peers, an instinctual control over magic that baffled even the most seasoned instructors. She excelled in everything they threw at her—elemental manipulation, warding spells, even advanced transmutations that stumped other students. It was as if the magic flowed through her without resistance, bending to her will as easily as breathing.

"Perhaps the firestorm wasn't so far-fetched after all," Kandor had mused during their latest lesson. While watching her create a swirling vortex of flame that hovered above her hand with startling precision, he explained how Tether flowed from their planes through the monoliths and obelisks around Valdessia. How she was a sort of enigma, how she seemed to have a connection to all the planes, which was extremely unusual.

Despite her growing recognition, the weight of her isolation never lifted. Other students watched her with a mix of awe and unease, whispering about her in hushed tones but rarely speaking to her directly. She tried to socialize, to make small talk between classes or in the dining hall, but the conversations always fizzled, and the gaps between her and the others seemed to grow wider each day.

The only place she felt any warmth was in her private conversations with Tara. The princess had remained her steadfast friend, though her visits had become more infrequent as her royal duties pulled her away. Amaura clung to those moments, hoping that one day she would find other connections, real friendships that weren't built on obligation or awe.

One evening, after a long day of study and practice, Amaura returned to the modest room she shared with her sister. Tryphena sat by the hearth, a faint smile on her lips as she saw Amaura enter.

"How was it today?" Tryphena asked, her tone light but laced with genuine interest.

Amaura shrugged, though her eyes glowed with the excitement she didn't quite know how to express. "Good. I learned a new binding spell in Professor Saelis' class. And Master Elandor... he's starting to believe me about the firestorm."

Tryphena chuckled softly. "It's about time. You've been showing them all up from the moment you stepped foot in that place."

Amaura sat down beside her sister, her gaze flickering toward the flames. "I'm getting better. But it still feels... I don't know, like no matter what I do, I'm always going to be 'the Aborrent.'"

"You're excelling, Amaura. That's what matters," Tryphena said, her voice soft but firm. "But you can't do this for them. You can't spend your life trying to prove yourself to people who will always find a reason to look down on you."

Amaura looked at her, a flicker of confusion crossing her face. "Then who am I supposed to do it for?"

"For yourself," Tryphena replied, her expression hardening. "You've always had power, more than you even realize. But you have to own it, not let them shape it. If you let others dictate why you use your magic, you'll end up like we were before—controlled, used."

Amaura flinched at the memory of their former life, of the mental chains they had worn under their old mistress's cruel hand. She had sworn never to return to that, but the fear of it lingered, like a shadow that refused to lift.

"I don't want to be used," she said quietly. "But... I just want them to accept me."

Tryphena leaned forward, her gaze intense. "They'll only accept you if you bend to their expectations. And if you do that, Amaura, you'll lose the part of yourself that makes you strong. Power like yours... it's a gift, but also a burden. Don't give it away for approval."

Amaura stared into the flames, her sister's words sinking in. She wanted so badly to fit in, to be more than just the girl with the pale skin and white hair that everyone whispered about. But Tryphena was right. Power like hers had been earned through suffering, and she couldn't let anyone take that from her.

She looked back at her sister, a new resolve forming. "You're right. I'll keep growing, but for me. Not for them."

Tryphena's smile returned, proud and fierce. "That's my sister. You've already come so far, Amaura. And there's so much more you'll accomplish. Just don't lose yourself along the way."

Amaura nodded, feeling a weight lift from her shoulders. She didn't know if she would ever truly belong at the Academy or if the whispers would ever stop. But she would keep moving forward—learning, growing, not for anyone else's approval but her own.

Tara leaned back in her chair, her eyes drifting to the window where the skyline of Aurelia's Hold stretched out, its towers bathed in the fading light of the afternoon. Across from her, Grayson tore into a hunk of bread with the same focus he gave to battle plans, his plate littered with the remains of their shared meal. The atmosphere was surprisingly relaxed—no royal ceremony, no formal setting, just two people having a quiet conversation over a modest dinner in her private quarters. It wasn't often Tara had time for such moments.

"I've been thinking," Tara began, pushing a stray lock of hair behind her ear. "If we're going to make your task force work, we need a faster way to move you around. Rainecourt isn't exactly small, and with the way things are going... Well, I think it's time we acquire an airship for your team's exclusive use."

Grayson raised an eyebrow, a bit of bread still in his hand. "An airship? For us?" He whistled low. "You're not holding back."

"I'm not in the habit of doing things halfway," she replied with a grin. "You'll need it. There's been a sharp rise in sky pirate activity, especially in the borderlands. My sources say it might be connected to Blake—he's up to something."

At the mention of Blake's name, Grayson's expression darkened, and Tara immediately regretted bringing him up. It was still a sore wound for both of them—Blake's betrayal and Commander Marzin's death were fresh in their minds. But this was exactly why they needed to act. If Blake was behind the attacks, Grayson's team would be the first to know, and they needed to stop him before he caused more damage.

"Sky pirates," Grayson said, wiping his hands and leaning forward. "That complicates things. Pirates alone are bad enough, but if Blake's pulling strings..."

"I want your team to investigate the attacks. Find out who's behind them, stop them if you can. But be careful. We don't know the full extent of their network, and I won't have you risking your life without backup."

Grayson nodded, though his eyes remained thoughtful. "We're almost ready to go. The team's shaping up—finally—but I won't lie, getting everyone on board has been... a process."

Tara raised her brows. "Oh? What kind of 'process' are we talking about?"

A wry smile tugged at Grayson's lips. "Well, Katura practically laughed in my face when I mentioned the uniform. Said she wasn't going to wear anything 'formal' that would 'restrict her freedom of movement.' Took me three days and some very careful persuasion to convince her to at least agree to the cloak."

Tara snorted. "I'm not surprised. I'm guessing you let her win?"

"Of course. The cloak was a compromise." He chuckled. "And Jai? He threatened to leave the city entirely. Claimed he'd be halfway across the continent by now if I kept trying to tie him down. Took Yulen and I both to convince him this job could open more doors for him. Not easy with that one."

"I wouldn't expect it to be," Tara replied, her voice softening as she thought about how odd the team had seemed at first, but how perfectly they'd come together during the mission to Bloodstone. "But you managed it. They're all still here, aren't they?"

"Barely." Grayson shook his head. "But I have to admit, I think they're coming around. Maybe they actually want to be a part of something bigger than themselves." He glanced at her then, something unreadable in his expression. "You know, it's strange. They're not the most conventional group, but somehow... it works."

Tara smiled, feeling a small swell of pride. "That's why I picked them. I knew they were the right fit."

"Sure, if by 'right fit' you mean a loose collection of misfits who could break into an argument at any second."

"It adds character," she teased, taking a sip of her drink. "Keeps you on your toes."

Grayson snorted. "That it does." He paused, a small smile creeping onto his face. "You know, if I didn't know any better, I'd say you're enjoying watching me struggle to wrangle them."

Tara gave him a look of mock innocence. "Me? Enjoying your suffering? Never."

"Oh, you are. I can tell. Every time I come to you with another disaster, you get that little smirk like you're thinking, 'I told him it wouldn't be easy.'"

She couldn't help the laugh that bubbled out. "Maybe I just enjoy the challenge. Watching you rise to it."

Grayson leaned back in his chair, crossing his arms as he regarded her. "Is that it? Or is it that you enjoy having me running around, doing all your dirty work?"

"Well, I wasn't going to say it, but now that you mention it..." Tara bit back a smile, realizing how relaxed she felt in his company. They had worked well together from the start, but there was something different now, something lighter about the way they bantered. For a moment, it felt as though the weight of the kingdom had lifted from her shoulders.

And then it hit her.

This was beginning to feel like a date.

Tara's stomach tightened at the thought, and she quickly looked down at her plate, suddenly embarrassed. This wasn't a date. It was a meeting—discussing strategy, their plans for the task force. Nothing more. Grayson was her friend. Her trusted confidant. She couldn't afford to think of him like that, not with everything else they had on their shoulders.

But her heart didn't quite get the message.

Grayson, oblivious to her sudden shift in mood, continued. "Anyway, I think we're close. Katura's not going to wear the uniform exactly, but she agreed to the colors and she'll fight. Jai's sticking around—for now. Yulen's always been solid, so no worries there. Starc and Tomas are easy sells. I'll keep them in line."

"I trust you will," she said, recovering her composure. "But I meant what I said. Be careful. This task force... it's not just about defending Rainecourt. It's about keeping all of you alive, too. And I can't afford to lose any of you."

Grayson's expression softened at that, his usual bravado fading for a moment. "You won't lose us, princess."

"Tara," she corrected quietly.

Grayson smirked, the tension easing as quickly as it had risen. "Right. Tara." He stood, pushing his chair back. "I'll get the team ready. As soon as the airship's ours, we'll be ready to move."

Tara watched him as he walked toward the door, her heart still fluttering in her chest. She needed to shake this feeling off. There was too much at stake—her kingdom, the pirates, Blake. But as Grayson paused and turned back to look at her, his smile lingering, she knew it wouldn't be that easy.

"Don't work too hard," he called. "You deserve a break every once in a while."

"I'll keep that in mind," she replied, her voice softer than she intended.

As the door closed behind him, Tara let out a breath she hadn't realized she was holding. This wasn't a date. It couldn't be.

But it felt dangerously close.

Amaura sat beneath the shade of a large oak in the Academy's courtyard, her pale hands folded in her lap as she stared blankly at the fountain ahead of her. The gentle sound of water splashing onto the stone should have been calming, but her head was swimming. Her vision blurred around the edges, and a wave of dizziness forced her to grip the ground for stability.

It had been too long since she last drank any blood.

Tara had been her reliable source, visiting regularly with a warm smile and a small flask, always ensuring she never went too long without. But it had been nearly two weeks since the last visit. Tara must have gotten busy, caught up in her royal duties, and though Amaura understood, it didn't make the gnawing hunger any easier to bear.

She hated this feeling—the desperate, instinctual need that bubbled up inside her. It made her feel monstrous, like the thing people whispered about when they looked at her too long.

A shadow fell over her, and she blinked up to see Grayson standing above her, his arms crossed. His rough features softened as he crouched down to her level, concern evident in his gaze.

"You look like hell, Amaura," he said bluntly, though his tone was laced with a touch of humor. "Everything alright?"

Amaura managed a weak smile. "Just a little lightheaded."

Grayson's brow furrowed as he studied her. "Lightheaded, huh? That wouldn't have anything to do with a certain princess being too busy to stop by, would it?"

Her face warmed, and she glanced away, embarrassed. "She's... she has responsibilities. It's fine."

Grayson shook his head, sitting down beside her on the cool grass. "It's not fine if you're about to keel over."

She stiffened at his words, unsure of how much he understood about her condition. She hadn't exactly advertised it, and Tara had kept it discreet, but Grayson had always been perceptive. Before she could say anything, he reached into his pack and pulled out a small canteen, twisting the cap off.

"It's not royal blood," he joked, holding it out to her. "But I figure it's decent quality. Filled the canteen just last night, when I heard how long it'd been since Tara dropped by."

Amaura's breath caught in her throat. The offer startled her, more because it was so casual—so... kind. She stared at the canteen for a moment too long, the hunger in her stomach twisting painfully, but her hesitation was stronger. She didn't want him to see her like this, didn't want him to think of her as just some monster that drank blood to survive.

"I—" She shook her head, trying to push the canteen back toward him. "I can't. I don't want you to…"

"To what?" Grayson raised an eyebrow, his expression curious but not judgmental. "Think less of you?"

She bit her lip, not daring to meet his gaze.

Grayson let out a quiet sigh, leaning back against the tree as if recalling an old memory. "You know, once, when I was trapped in an underground ruin beneath Komu, I had to live off raw rats for nearly two weeks. Best protein I could get at the time." He paused, glancing at her to see if she was listening. "Wasn't exactly gourmet dining, but I did what I had to. Kept me alive. Now, tell me something—would you judge me for that?"

Amaura blinked, turning her head toward him. "Of course not."

"Then why would I judge you for doing what you need to survive?" Grayson's eyes were steady, sincere. He gave her a small, reassuring smile. "You're not a monster, Amaura. You're just someone who's got a little bit of a different need than most people. That's all."

The knot in her chest loosened slightly at his words, but still, she hesitated. Grayson sensed her reluctance and softened his voice further.

"Look, I'm not offering because I feel sorry for you. I'm offering because I want to help, and because you're part of the team—even if you're not officially on it, yet." He winked, holding the canteen out once more. "And if you faint in the middle of the courtyard, that's going to be a lot more embarrassing than just taking a sip now."

She couldn't help but laugh softly at that, the sound dry but real. Grayson had a way of cutting through her reservations, disarming her with his straightforwardness. Reluctantly, Amaura reached for the canteen, her fingers brushing his as she took it.

"Thank you," she whispered, unscrewing the cap and lifting it to her lips.

The first sip sent a wave of warmth through her, a rush of strength returning to her limbs. The blood was sweet, a taste that surprised her, and with each swallow, the dizziness faded. Her pale cheeks flushed with new energy, her heart settling into a steadier rhythm. She drank slowly, not wanting to overdo it, and when she finally lowered the canteen, she let out a long breath of relief.

Grayson watched her with a grin. "Feeling better?"

She nodded, grateful but unsure how to express it. "I—yes, I do. It… it helps. Thank you, Grayson."

"Good to hear." He capped the canteen and tucked it away. "I was actually looking for you, anyway. Wanted to check in before I head out on a mission. Might be gone for a bit."

Amaura's brow furrowed. "A mission?"

"Yeah. Tara's got me chasing down sky pirates. We're putting together a team to deal with them, see if we can figure out who's been pulling the strings." He shrugged as if it were no big deal, but she knew it was a dangerous task.

"I hope you'll be careful," she said, her voice too gentle for the stern warning she'd intended.

Grayson gave her a playful smirk. "You're starting to sound like the princess."

Amaura smiled shyly. "Maybe I've been spending too much time with her."

"I wouldn't call that a bad thing." He leaned forward, resting his elbows on his knees. "Actually, once you're done with your studies here, I was hoping you'd consider joining my task force."

Her eyes widened in surprise. "You... you want me to join?"

"Of course," Grayson said, as if it were the most obvious thing in the world. "You're a powerful mage, smart and loyal. Everyone's going to be throwing recruitment offers your way, trust me. But I'd like to call dibs." He winked, his tone lighthearted, but there was a charming sincerity beneath it.

She stared at him for a moment, stunned by the compliment. Her heart fluttered, and suddenly, she felt something unexpected—a warmth that wasn't from the blood. Grayson had always been kind to her, but now, sitting beside him, the way he spoke to her with such ease and familiarity, it stirred something deeper. He wasn't just a rescuer, a protector. He was... something more.

"I... I'll think about it," she replied, her voice almost shy.

"You do that," he said with a grin. "But don't take too long. I'm telling you, offers are going to be flooding in soon enough."

As they sat in the courtyard, the sun slowly dipping below the horizon, Amaura found herself looking at Grayson in a new light. He wasn't just a warrior or a leader—he was someone who made her feel seen, not as a monster, but as a person.

And for the first time since coming to Aurelia's Hold, she wondered if maybe, just maybe, she was starting to feel something more than gratitude for him.

Chapter 10

Nestled in the Gilded Ridge, the mountain village of Emberstone lay in ruins, its cobblestone streets scattered with the smoldering remains of homes and market stalls. The air was thick with the acrid stench of burning wood and something sharper, darker—blood, Grayson guessed, though the ground was curiously free of bodies. His boots crunched against shattered pottery as he stepped forward, scanning the destruction with a practiced eye. Famed forges that crafted weapons for Raincourts' armies lay in ruins, shattering the image of a once proud and vibrant town.

Katura knelt beside a splintered wagon, her sharp eyes studying the scorch marks on its frame. "This wasn't a typical raid," she murmured, running her fingers over the charred wood. "They burned everything they couldn't carry, but ... it's too clean. They left nothing behind."

"Clean isn't the word I'd use," Jai muttered, arms crossed as he surveyed the wreckage from a safe distance. "More like... clinical. Precise."

Grayson's gaze shifted to the cluster of villagers gathered near the remnants of the village square. Most looked shell-shocked, their faces pale and hollow as they whispered among themselves. A few braver souls had stepped forward to speak with him, their expressions grim.

One of them, an older man with a heavy limp, stood clutching a crude walking stick. His face was etched with lines that spoke of years of hard labor, but his eyes were red and swollen from recent grief. "It was them sky pirates," he said, his voice shaking with equal parts anger and despair. "Came down from the clouds in their cursed ship. Fast as a storm, they were. We didn't stand a chance."

Grayson nodded, gesturing for the man to continue. "How many were there?"

"Dozens," the man replied. "Maybe more. They moved like they knew every corner of the village. Went straight for the livestock, the grain stores. And... and the people."

Another villager, a woman clutching a soot-streaked shawl, stepped forward. "They killed anyone who resisted," she said, her voice brittle. "Didn't matter if it was a man or a child. They had no mercy."

Grayson's jaw tightened. He'd seen the aftermath of pirate raids before, but something about this felt... wrong. He glanced around again, taking in the absence of bodies. "What about the ones they killed?" he asked. "Where are they?"

The villagers exchanged uneasy glances before the older man answered. "They... they took them."

Grayson frowned. "They took the dead?"

"Aye," the man said, nodding grimly. "Loaded them up like cargo. We saw them—lifeless bodies, some still bleeding. They piled them onto their ship like they were worth something."

Katura straightened, her expression hard. "Are you sure they were dead?" she asked. "Not just unconscious or injured?"

"They were dead," the woman insisted, her grip tightening on her shawl. "I saw my husband's body with my own eyes. His throat was slit. There was no life left in him."

Grayson felt a chill creep up his spine. Pirates capturing slaves was one thing—vile, but predictable. But taking the dead? That was something else entirely. His mind raced, trying to piece together what it could mean.

"What could they possibly want with dead bodies?" Jai asked, voicing the question that hung heavy in the air.

"Nothing good," Grayson said, his voice grim. "That's for sure."

If Blake was involved—and Grayson had little doubt that he was—then this was more than just a raid for supplies or slaves. This was calculated, deliberate, and whatever they were planning, it wasn't going to stop here.

He turned back to the villagers. "How long ago did they leave?"

"Two days," the old man said. "Maybe three. They moved fast. Once they had what they wanted, they vanished into the sky."

Grayson nodded, with an unreadable expression. "We'll find them," he promised, his voice firm. "And we'll make sure they don't come back."

The villagers murmured their gratitude, though their eyes were still heavy with despair. Grayson didn't blame them. Promises of vengeance were cold comfort when your home lay in ruins and your loved ones had been stolen—or worse.

As the team regrouped, Katura stepped closer, her voice low. "I have a feeling this is bigger than just pirates. We'll need more than just us."

"I know," Grayson said shortly. It said something that even Katura couldn't help but feel the gravity of the situation. "But for now, we track them. Figure out where they're going, what they're planning."

"And if we find them?" Jai asked.

Grayson's gaze was hard as steel. "Then we stop them. Whatever it takes."

The battlefield was eerily quiet in the skirmish's aftermath, save for the crackling of a smoldering wagon and the distant groans of defeated pirates sprawled across the rocky terrain of The Verdant Peaks. Grayson wiped blood from his blade and sheathed it, his gaze locking onto the pirate commander pinned beneath Yulen's heavy knee. The man struggled fruitlessly, his face contorted with fury and defiance.

"Comfortable?" Yulen asked dryly, his gauntleted hand pressing harder on the pirate's shoulder.

"Go to hell," the pirate spat, glaring up at them with bloodshot eyes. His lip was split, his face streaked with dirt and sweat, but his spirit remained unbroken.

Grayson crouched down, his voice calm but edged with menace. "We've already been through hell, so I'll take that as an invitation to get cozy. Now, let's make this easy. Who's backing your crew? Is it Blake?"

The pirate smirked, blood staining his teeth. "Wouldn't you like to know?"

Grayson's jaw tightened. He hated dealing with the cocky ones—the ones whose loyalty to their crew or fear of their employer was stronger than the will to survive. He glanced at Yulen, who merely shrugged, without relenting on his grip.

Katura stepped forward with feather-light footsteps. Her daggers were sheathed at her sides, and her expression was a mask of disarming charm. She knelt beside the pirate, hovering with her face inches from his. "You've got quite the attitude for someone in your position," she said, adopting a low, sultry voice.

The pirate raised an eyebrow, a flicker of confusion crossing his features. "What're you—"

Katura smiled, tilting her head. "I think we can be friends, don't you?"

Before he could answer, her fingers traced intricate patterns in the air, glowing glyphs materializing around her hand. They shimmered with faint light before settling onto the pirate's face, spreading like ink across his skin. His defiance melted away almost instantly, replaced by wide-eyed adoration.

"My lady," the pirate murmured, his voice suddenly soft, reverent. "You're... incredible."

Katura leaned in closer, her smile widening. "I know. Now, sweetheart, I need you to do something for me. Answer Grayson's questions. Every single one. Can you do that for me?"

The pirate nodded fervently, his earlier bravado completely gone. "Anything for you."

Grayson raised an eyebrow at Katura, but she simply waved him off with a smirk. "Ask away, boss."

Grayson hesitated only a moment before leaning back toward the pirate. "Blake. He's backing you, isn't he?"

The pirate nodded eagerly. "Yeah. Blake's been giving weapons, coin, whatever we need. Says if we fight under his flag, we'll be unstoppable and have all the coin we could ever handle."

"And what's he planning?" Grayson pressed. "Why's he funding all these raids?"

"Not sure exactly," the pirate admitted, though his tone was far more cooperative now. "All I know is, he wants chaos. The more we disrupt the kingdom, the better it is for him. He's got people all over, ready to move when he gives the word."

Grayson exchanged a quick glance with Yulen, who nodded grimly. This was confirmation of what they'd suspected: Blake wasn't just raiding for the sake of it. He was building something bigger.

"And the bodies?" Grayson asked, his voice sharp. "Why's he collecting them?"

At that, the pirate's expression shifted, his infatuation with Katura momentarily giving way to fear. His eyes darted nervously, and his breath quickened. "I... I don't know."

Grayson narrowed his eyes. "You don't know, or you won't say?"

"I swear, I don't know!" the pirate exclaimed, trembling under Yulen's grip. "All I know is, it's not just loot he's after. He's got a... a 'special project,' he calls it. No one knows what it is, but—"

"But what?" Grayson demanded.

The pirate swallowed hard. "The last guy who asked too many questions? Blake pushed him off the airship without a second thought. No one asks about the bodies anymore."

Grayson's stomach churned at the thought, but he kept his composure. He leaned back, his mind racing. Whatever Blake was planning, it was bigger than simple piracy. Necromancy? A weapon? Something else entirely? They needed to find out.

"Where were you supposed to meet him next?" Grayson asked.

"In the mountains," the pirate replied, his voice trembling. "There's a spot just past the Redridge Pass. We were supposed to deliver our share of the loot there in three days."

Grayson nodded, rising to his feet. "The Azure Peaks. Good. That's all we need."

The pirate looked up at Katura, his expression pleading. "Did I do good? Are we... are we friends now?"

Katura patted his cheek lightly, her smirk returning. "Oh, you were perfect."

With a flick of her fingers, the glyphs on his face dissipated, leaving him disoriented and blinking in confusion. Grayson gave her a hard look, but she shrugged innocently. "What? It worked, didn't it?"

"Let's just hope the information is good," Grayson muttered, motioning for Yulen to release the pirate. "Tie him up with the others. We've got a lot to do."

As Yulen dragged the pirate away, Grayson turned to his team, his expression grim. "We head for Redridge Pass at first light. If Blake's there, we need to be ready for anything."

The group nodded, their usual banter absent in the wake of what they'd just learned. Grayson's gut told him they were walking into something far more dangerous than any of them had anticipated. And whatever Blake was doing with those bodies, it wasn't going to be good.

The Academy's garden courtyard was alive with the hum of lunchtime activity—students gathered at tables scattered under leafy canopies, sharing food and laughter. Tara sat across from Amaura at a secluded corner table, the soft murmur of conversation and the occasional burst of laughter providing a pleasant backdrop. The princess smiled as she unwrapped a small parcel of bread and cheese she'd brought with her.

"I'm sorry I haven't been able to visit more often," Tara said, her voice tinged with guilt. "Things at the palace have been... hectic. As if tracking down these pirates wasn't enough, now they are throwing bureaucratic crap my way. Princess, there are missing funds. Princess this Princess that." Tara threw her hands up as if surrendering and let out a deep sigh. "Although it helps me to appreciate the time I do have with my friends." She gave a relaxed and comforting smile to Amaura.

Amaura shook her head, her white hair catching the sunlight like spun silver. "You don't have to apologize. You're a princess; I know you have responsibilities. Besides, I've barely had time to think about anything outside my classes and practice."

Tara leaned forward slightly, her tone teasing. "Oh? Have they been working you that hard?"

Amaura's lips quirked into a small smile. "You could say that. Professor Saelis is relentless. And Master Elandor? He keeps finding new ways to test me, always saying I need to push beyond my limits." She paused, taking a sip from her cup of tea. "It's exhausting, but... I think I'm starting to find my footing."

"That doesn't surprise me," Tara said warmly. "You've always had a quiet strength about you, Amaura. It's no wonder you're excelling."

Amaura blushed slightly, her gaze dropping to her plate. "Thank you. That means a lot."

They ate in companionable silence for a few moments, the light breeze rustling the leaves overhead. Eventually, Tara broke the quiet. "I got a message from Grayson recently."

Amaura perked up, her interest piqued. "Oh? How is he?"

"He's got a lead," Tara replied, her tone equal parts pride and worry. "He thinks they're close to getting to the bottom of the situation with the pirates. If all goes well, he'll have answers soon."

"That's good," Amaura said, though her brow furrowed slightly. "But it's Grayson. 'If all goes well' isn't exactly his style."

Tara laughed, the sound light and musical. "You're right. He'll probably walk straight into danger without a second thought."

"Absolutely," Amaura agreed, her smile growing. "He seems to think he's invincible sometimes."

"Well," Tara said with a smirk, "he hasn't been proven wrong yet."

They both chuckled, though the underlying concern for his safety lingered in their expressions. Amaura's fingers traced the edge of her cup absently as she glanced at Tara. "He's... different, isn't he?"

Tara tilted her head, curious. "Different how?"

Amaura hesitated, searching for the right words. "I don't know. He has this way of... making you feel seen. Like he doesn't just look at what's on the surface, but he sees who you are underneath it all."

Tara's smile softened, and for a moment, her gaze grew distant. "Yeah. He does, doesn't he? He has this knack for cutting through all the noise and getting to the heart of things. It's one of the reasons I trust him so much."

Amaura nodded, her cheeks warming slightly. "He's... well, he's Grayson."

Tara laughed again, the sound a touch more nervous this time. "He is. Always charging headfirst into whatever challenge lies ahead, somehow making it all work out."

Amaura watched Tara carefully, her own curiosity piqued. "You talk about him a lot."

Tara blinked, then quickly shook her head. "I... well, he's my most trusted knight. I have to talk about him. He's out there risking his life for all of us."

Amaura smiled faintly, leaning back in her chair. "Of course."

They both fell silent, each lost in her own thoughts. Amaura stirred her tea absently, her mind drifting to the way Grayson had looked at her the last time they spoke, how he had reassured her so easily. Meanwhile, Tara toyed with the edge of her napkin, recalling Grayson's smirk when he'd teased her about overworking herself.

Finally, Tara broke the quiet. "You think he'll be alright, don't you?"

Amaura looked up, her expression soft but resolute. "He's Grayson. If anyone can walk into danger and come out the other side, it's him."

Tara nodded, her worry easing just a fraction. "You're right."

For a moment, they both smiled, neither realizing the other was thinking of Grayson in the same way —with a mix of admiration, gratitude, and something that was slowly blooming into something deeper.

The conversation shifted back to lighter topics after that—classes, palace gossip, and academy rumors—but the unspoken feelings lingered beneath the surface, unnoticed by both but perhaps not as hidden as either believed.

The Azure Peaks made sense that Blake would have a hideout there. The Isle of Lynthara was off the eastern coast and while it is a part of Raincourt, that region always kept to themselves quiet and unassuming. The mountain pass was eerily quiet, the sharp wind biting at Grayson's face as he surveyed the empty clearing. His team spread out behind him, combing through the site for any clue, but the scene was barren. The ground bore faint traces of activity—trampled grass, a half-extinguished firepit, and a few discarded scraps of cloth. Whoever had been here had left in a hurry, covering their tracks well.

Grayson's jaw clenched as frustration bubbled to the surface. It had been over a month since they'd left the capital, chasing one lead after another, only to find themselves repeatedly arriving too late. This rendezvous site had been their best chance yet to catch someone connected to Blake's operation. And now, yet again, the enemy had slipped through their fingers.

"Nothing," Katura called, walking up with her hands on her hips. "Whoever was here, they cleared out fast. No supplies, no clues—just empty space."

"They must've known we were coming," Yulen said, his voice grim as he approached from the opposite side of the clearing. "Maybe someone tipped them off."

Grayson gritted his teeth, his hand tightening around the hilt of his sword. "Or they've got scouts. They could've seen us coming a mile away in this terrain."

Jai sauntered over, shaking his head. "This is starting to feel like a bad joke. How many more wild goose chases are we going to go on before we actually catch someone?"

Grayson didn't respond, his frustration too raw for words. He scanned the horizon, his eyes narrowing as he tried to piece together what they were missing. The cold wind whistled through the pass, carrying with it the faint scent of ash from the long-dead fire.

Tomas, who had been crouched near the firepit, finally stood and turned toward them. "Wait a second," he said, his voice cutting through the tension. "The Tether. I can sense it—there's been recent activity here."

Grayson turned to him, his expression sharpening. "What kind of activity?"

"Messages," Tomas said, his tone certain as he waved a hand, faint trails of energy glimmering in the air around him. "Someone's been using the Tether to communicate. Back and forth. It's faint, but it's there. They must've used it not long ago, probably when they realized we were on our way."

Grayson's frustration gave way to cautious hope. "Can you track it?"

Tomas nodded slowly, his brow furrowing in concentration. "It'll take time. The trails are faint, and the magic they used was... deliberate. But if I focus, I might be able to figure out where the messages were sent to—or who sent them."

"How much time?" Grayson asked, his tone urgent.

"An hour, maybe two," Tomas replied. "If we're lucky."

Grayson looked around the clearing, his team watching him expectantly. The cold, the emptiness, the endless pursuit—it was all wearing on them. But this was their first real lead in weeks, and he wasn't about to let it slip away.

"Do it," he said, his voice firm. "Whatever you need, we'll give you the time."

Tomas nodded and knelt again, his hands glowing faintly as he began to weave a complex pattern in the air. The glyphs shimmered and danced, aligning with the faint traces of the Tether that lingered in the clearing. The rest of the team spread out, keeping watch as Grayson stood nearby, his arms crossed and his mind racing.

If this worked, they might finally have a way to get to Blake—or whoever was pulling the strings behind this madness. Grayson clenched his fists, his frustration fueling his determination. They had been chasing shadows for too long. It was time to bring this to an end.

Chapter 11

T he *Enduring* crested the rugged side of the mountain range, its engines humming steadily as it followed the narrow path Tomas had charted. The airship's gleaming hull reflected the setting sun, and the steady rhythm of its propellers filled the crisp, thin air. Grayson stood on the deck, his hands gripping the rail as he scanned the jagged peaks ahead.

Tomas's voice came through the comm crystal clipped to Grayson's belt. "The Tether trail is getting stronger. We're close. Another few miles, maybe less."

"Good," Grayson replied, his tone clipped but resolute. "We've been chasing this for long enough."

Before Tomas could respond, a deafening *BOOM* echoed through the mountains, followed by a sharp whistle and then a thunderous impact. The airship lurched violently, the deck tilting beneath Grayson's feet as he grabbed the rail to steady himself.

"What the hell was that?" Jai shouted, running up from below deck.

"Anti-air artillery!" the pilot's voice crackled over the same comm crystal. "Cannons hidden in the mountains—port side took a hit!"

Another explosion rocked the ship, this time closer. Smoke billowed from one of the starboard fins, and the ship jerked sharply as the pilot banked hard to avoid further fire. Grayson gritted his teeth as the deck tilted again, the sound of alarms blaring through the airship.

"Well," Grayson muttered, his voice grim as he steadied himself. "At least we know we're in the right place."

Katura appeared beside him, her expression a mix of amusement and annoyance. "Glad you're finding the silver lining in all this, boss."

"We've been shot at before," he replied, casting her a quick smirk. "This isn't new."

Jai grabbed onto the rail, looking less thrilled. "Yeah, but most of the time, the ground isn't several thousand feet below us."

"Pilot," Grayson called into the comm crystal, "get us out of range. Tomas, you know the drill. Stay with the ship and keep us all in contact. And keep a focus on the Tether trail. Don't want to be wandering blind through these mountains."

"Understood," Tomas replied, his voice steady despite the chaos around him.

"Yulen, Katura, Jai, Starc—you're with me," Grayson said, his voice firm. "Gear up and get to the skyskiff. We're going in."

The team moved quickly, grabbing their weapons and equipment as the *Enduring* tilted again, the pilot skillfully maneuvering the ship to avoid another round of fire. Grayson led the way to the aft section, where the sleek skyskiff was docked—a smaller, more agile vessel designed for rapid deployment. Its frame gleamed with reinforced plating, and its twin engines hummed with readiness.

The team piled into the skyskiff, securing themselves as Grayson took the controls. Starc, their gunner, manned the forward turret, his fingers twitching with anticipation. The skyskiff detached from the *Enduring* with a sharp *CLUNK*, the engines roaring to life as Grayson guided it away from the larger airship.

"Hold on," Grayson called over his shoulder, gripping the controls tightly. "This is going to get bumpy."

The skyskiff shot forward, weaving through the mountain peaks as explosions erupted around them. Starc returned fire, aiming at the hidden artillery emplacements, while Jai kept his eyes on the landscape ahead, scanning for any sign of their target.

"Any updates, Tomas?" Grayson asked through the comm.

"The trail's still strong," Tomas replied, his voice calm but urgent. "Keep heading north—there's a narrow pass just ahead. That's where it's leading."

Grayson nodded, focusing on the path ahead. The mountains loomed closer, the jagged cliffs casting long shadows in the fading light. The skyskiff's engines whined as it pushed through the turbulence, the team bracing themselves as Grayson guided the vessel into the narrow pass Tomas had described.

As they entered the pass, the artillery fire lessened, the cliffs providing some cover. Grayson's jaw tightened as he maneuvered the skyskiff through the winding terrain. "Get ready, everyone. If they've got this much firepower protecting the area, whatever's here is important."

"And probably crawling with hostiles," Yulen added, his voice gruff but steady as he checked his gear.

Grayson kept his focus on the controls. "Let's make this count. We've got one chance to hit them before they scatter again."

As the skyskiff flew deeper into the mountains, the air grew colder, the tension palpable. Grayson's team, seasoned and battle-hardened, prepared themselves for whatever lay ahead. For the first time in weeks, it felt like they were finally closing in on their elusive enemy—and Grayson wasn't about to let them slip away again.

The skyskiff weaved through the narrow mountain pass, its engines roaring as Grayson pushed it to its limits. The serrated cliffs loomed on either side, and the occasional burst of artillery fire echoed through the air, shaking the small vessel.

"There!" Jai shouted, pointing to the left. "Cannon emplacement, two o'clock, halfway up the cliff!"

Grayson adjusted the skyskiff, bringing it into position as Starc swiveled the forward turret. The barrel locked onto the cannon's position, and with a sharp pull of the trigger, the glyph glowed and a burst of energy shot from the gun, striking the artillery. The explosion lit up the mountainside, sending debris cascading down the cliff face.

"Nice shot, Starc!" Jai called, a grin breaking through the tension.

But the victory was short-lived. The skyskiff shuddered violently as another artillery round struck it from the side, the explosion rocking the vessel and sending it into a chaotic spin.

"Brace yourselves!" Grayson yelled, gripping the controls desperately. The skyskiff plummeted, its engines sputtering as it careened toward the mountainside.

The crash was deafening. Metal screamed against rock as the skyskiff slammed into the ground, skidding across the uneven terrain before coming to a jarring halt. Dust and debris filled the air, and for a moment, all was still.

Grayson groaned, pushing himself upright and assessing the situation. Starc was already pulling himself free from the wreckage, his usually calm expression grim. Jai was kneeling over Yulen, who lay motionless amidst the debris, his massive form eerily still.

"Yulen!" Jai's voice cracked as he shook the oni's shoulder. "Come on, big guy, wake up! Why do you have to be so damn selfless!" Jai looked up at the group, fighting back a swelling of emotions for his friend. "He pushed me aside, he…"

Grayson moved over, crouching beside them. Yulen's chest rose and fell slowly, but his eyes remained closed, and a deep gash across his temple bled sluggishly. "He's alive," Grayson said, relief mingling with urgency. "But he's out cold."

Katura appeared at their side with a look of determination. She knelt beside Yulen, her hands glowing faintly as she summoned the Tether. The energy swirled around her fingers, weaving intricate patterns as she pressed her hands to Yulen's wound. "I can stabilize him," she said, her voice calm but firm. "But it's going to take time before he regains consciousness."

Jai hovered nearby, his expression a mixture of worry and guilt. "Are you sure he's going to be okay?"

"He's tougher than all of us combined," Katura replied with a small smile. "But even he's not invincible. Don't worry—I'll take care of him."

Grayson stood, his jaw tight as he surveyed the area. The skyskiff was a wreck, its frame twisted and engines smoking. They were grounded, and the crash site was far from secure. "We can't stay here," he said, his tone short. "Starc, Jai, you're with me. We'll continue on foot."

Jai hesitated, glancing back at Yulen, but Grayson placed a firm hand on his shoulder. "He's in good hands. Katura will catch up once he's stable."

Katura nodded, not breaking her focus as the Tether's energy pulsed beneath her hands. "Go. I'll make sure he's safe and then find you."

Grayson gave her a quick nod before turning to Starc and Jai. "Grab what you can from the wreckage. We move fast and quiet. If there are more emplacements or hostiles nearby, we don't want to give them time to regroup."

Within moments, the three of them were moving, their gear strapped to their backs and weapons at the ready. The jagged peaks loomed above them as they pressed onward, the cold wind biting at their faces. Grayson's mind raced as they pushed through the rugged terrain. The crash had been a setback, but they were close—he could feel it. Whatever Blake and his allies were hiding, they were on the verge of uncovering it.

Behind them, Katura continued her work, her hands steady as the Tether's glow enveloped Yulen's wounds. "Don't you dare leave me with all the heavy lifting, big guy," she muttered, her voice soft but determined. "You've still got a job to do."

The group pressed forward, the shadows of the mountains growing longer as the day wore on. Each step brought them closer to their goal—and to the danger that awaited them.

Grayson's team had barely made it past the first ridge when the ambush came. A deafening crack echoed through the mountains as the first shot rang out, the bullet ricocheting off a rock mere inches from Grayson's head. He ducked instinctively, dragging Jai and Starc with him as another volley of gunfire erupted from the cliffs above.

"Cover!" Grayson barked, diving behind a boulder as bullets sprayed the path. Starc crouched beside him, his expression grim, while Jai flattened himself against the mountain wall, scanning for a way out.

"There's at least a dozen of them!" Starc called, peeking out briefly before ducking back as a bullet zipped past. "All perched up high, too."

Grayson gritted his teeth, drawing his pistol and quickly assessing their position. The pirates had the advantage, firing from rocky ledges above, their rifles trained on the narrow path below. It was a kill box, and they were pinned.

"Jai!" Grayson shouted over the gunfire. "Think you can flank them?"

Jai looked furious as he drew his daggers. "You know it. Keep their eyes on you."

Grayson nodded and popped out from behind the boulder, firing off a few quick shots with his pistol. The sharp cracks of his gun echoed through the mountains, and a pirate cried out as one of Grayson's bullets found its mark. The return fire was immediate and furious, forcing him to duck back down, but it had done its job—the pirates' attention was squarely on him. Quickly ejecting his cartridge to check and refill his bullets, he thought, *there's your opening Jai.*

Jai moved like a shadow, slipping over the edge of the mountain path and disappearing below. Grayson fired again, his shots deliberate, drawing the pirates' fire toward him. Starc joined in, leaning out to fire his crossbow at one of the pirates above. The bolt struck true, and another rifleman toppled from his perch, his weapon clattering down the rocky slope.

Meanwhile, Jai crept along the ridge, his movements silent and precise. He reached the first pirate unseen, his dagger flashing in the dim light as he plunged it into the man's back. The pirate fell without a sound, and Jai moved on, his second blade ready.

The pirates above began to notice their numbers dwindling. One of them turned just in time to catch a glimpse of Jai as he dispatched another rifleman, and a shout of alarm went up. The remaining pirates began to split their focus, some firing at Grayson and Starc while others turned their rifles toward the rogue darting through their ranks.

Grayson saw Jai's cover slipping and took aim, his pistol barking twice in rapid succession. Both shots found their marks, dropping two of the pirates who had their sights on Jai. "Keep moving!" Grayson shouted, reloading his pistol with practiced speed. "I've got you!"

Jai gave him a quick nod, his expression never faltering as he slipped into the shadows again. The pirates were scrambling now, their ambush falling apart under the combined assault. Grayson picked off another with a clean shot to the shoulder, forcing the man to drop his rifle and retreat.

"Grayson!" Starc called suddenly, his voice urgent. "We've got company!"

Grayson turned just in time to see three pirates rounding the corner of the mountain path, their swords drawn as they charged toward him. He raised his pistol, but before he could fire, Starc stepped forward, his twin swords flashing in the fading light.

The first pirate swung wildly, but Starc sidestepped with ease, his left blade slicing across the man's chest. He spun on his heel, deflecting the second pirate's strike with one sword while driving the other into the man's gut. The third pirate hesitated, seeing his comrades fall, but Starc gave him no time to reconsider. With a quick feint and a decisive strike, the last swordsman fell, his weapon clattering to the ground.

Starc wiped his blades on his sleeve, his expression as calm as ever. "Clear on this end."

Grayson nodded, sparing him a brief smile before turning his attention back to the cliffs above. The remaining pirates were scattered and disorganized, their rifle fire sporadic. Another shot from Grayson's pistol sent one tumbling from his perch, and the last few began to flee, disappearing into the rocky terrain.

A moment later, Jai reappeared, climbing up to the path with a devilish smirk. "That went well," he said, sheathing his daggers. "I think we ruined their day."

"Not bad, Jai," Grayson said, holstering his pistol. "Nice work out there."

Starc glanced around, his sharp eyes scanning the area for any stragglers. "We should keep moving. If these were just the scouts, the rest of their crew might not be far."

Grayson nodded, his expression serious. "Agreed. Stay sharp, everyone. If this was just the welcome party, the main event's going to be worse."

The team regrouped, their steps quick and silent as they continued deeper into the mountains. The ambush had been a close call, but they were still standing—and they were getting closer to whatever Blake had hidden in the heart of these cliffs.

The mountain air grew colder as Grayson's group climbed higher, the wind carrying an unsettling silence. No further ambushes. No patrols. Nothing but the distant calls of mountain birds and the crunch of boots on gravel. It didn't sit right with Grayson.

"This doesn't feel right," he muttered, scanning the jagged peaks above. "If they were willing to throw a dozen riflemen at us earlier, why haven't we seen anyone else?"

"Maybe we scared them off," Starc offered, though his tone betrayed his own doubts.

Grayson shook his head. "No. These aren't the type to scare that easily. They're up to something." It didn't sit right with Grayson, and he brought the group to a halt.

Jai crouched nearby, his daggers glinting faintly as he adjusted his grip. "Want me to scout ahead?"

Grayson hesitated only a moment before nodding. "Keep to the shadows. Don't engage. Just get eyes on whatever's ahead."

Jai nodded. He had seemed more determined since the crash. "On it."

The rogue slipped into the shadows with practiced ease, his form blending seamlessly into the terrain. Grayson and Starc waited, the minutes stretching long as they watched the winding path. The mountain loomed above, its cliffs and ledges forming a natural fortress. Whatever Blake's people were hiding here, it was well-protected.

Jai returned after what felt like an eternity, his expression grim. He crouched beside Grayson and Starc, his voice low. "I found them. Main camp's up ahead, inside a cavern on the other side of the ridge."

"And?" Grayson prompted, already bracing for bad news.

Jai sighed. "There are dozens of them. Maybe more. They've fortified the entrance with barricades, and I spotted at least three sentry towers carved into the rock. No way we're taking that on with just the three of us."

Grayson's jaw tightened, his instincts warring with logic. "Blake might be in there. If we wait for backup, we risk him slipping away."

"And if we charge in now, we're dead," Starc said bluntly. "Even you can't take on a small army by yourself, Grayson."

Grayson exhaled sharply, his frustration evident. Every second they delayed felt like another step closer to losing their target, but Starc was right. A frontal assault would be suicide.

Grayson reached out to Tomas, confident they were still connected via Tether energy. "Tomas, come in."

The response was immediate. "I'm here. What's the situation?"

"We found the main camp," Grayson said. "Jai estimates there are dozens of them—too many for us to take on alone. We need reinforcements."

"Understood," Tomas replied. "The nearest military vessel is the *Skyward Blade*. They're stationed two hours south, patrolling the borderlands. I can send a message and have them redirect here."

"Do it," Grayson said. "Tell them to move fast. If Blake's in that camp, I don't want him slipping through our fingers."

"Consider it done," Tomas said. "And Grayson—stay alive."

Grayson allowed himself a faint smile. "That's the plan."

He turned to Jai and Starc. "We'll hold position until reinforcements arrive. Take perches along the mountain path—if anyone tries to make a run for it, we'll cut them off."

Jai nodded, already moving to find a suitable hiding spot. "I'll take the south ridge. Lots of cover there."

Starc hefted his swords, his eyes scanning the area. "I'll stick to the higher ground. If they come this way, they won't make it far."

Grayson climbed to a vantage point overlooking the path, his pistol drawn and ready. The minutes dragged by as he watched the mountain, his nerves coiled like a spring. The silence felt heavier now, each creak of a tree branch or rustle of loose stones making him tense.

As he scanned the horizon, his thoughts churned. Waiting was the smart call, but it didn't make it any easier. Blake had always been slippery, and if the man managed to escape again...

Grayson pushed the thought aside, forcing himself to focus. The mission wasn't over yet, and reinforcements were on the way. All they had to do was hold the line and make sure no one left that camp before the cavalry arrived.

The wind picked up, carrying faint sounds from the cavern in the distance—voices, movement. Grayson tightened his grip on his pistol and settled in for the wait, his mind sharp and ready for whatever came next. Eventually, the source of that sound caught his eye. A group of pirates was emerging from the direction of the cavern, moving quickly but cautiously along the winding trail. At their head was a hulking man, easily twice the size of the others. The weapon he carried immediately drew Grayson's attention—a massive, multi-barreled rifle that whirred ominously as the man adjusted his grip. Steam hissed from the pack on his back, which was connected to the rifle by a series of thick tubes.

"What the hell is that?" Grayson muttered, his stomach knotting as he realized the answer wasn't going to be good.

The hulking man stopped, leveling the weapon in Grayson's direction. The barrels spun rapidly, the steam pack on his back releasing a plume of vapor as the rifle roared to life. Bullets tore through the air in rapid succession, a hailstorm of lead that slammed into the rocks around Grayson's perch.

Grayson dove for cover, but the barrage was relentless. One of the shots struck him in the shoulder, the impact throwing him backward with a sharp cry of pain. He fell from his perch, tumbling down the rocky slope. The world spun wildly around him, and he barely managed to grab hold of an outcropping, his fingers scrabbling against the rough stone as he stopped just shy of sliding off the mountain path entirely.

Pain lanced through his shoulder, blood soaking into his jacket. He gritted his teeth, trying to pull himself up, but the relentless fire from the strange weapon pinned him down. From his precarious position, he could see Jai and Starc attempting to respond, but neither could get close enough to take a shot without exposing themselves to the deadly barrage.

"Damn it," Grayson hissed, sweat dripping into his eyes as the situation grew more dire. The pirates were advancing, the hulking man with the steam rifle grinning as he continued his assault. The weapon was like nothing Grayson had ever seen—deadly, efficient, and completely overpowering.

Just as Grayson began to fear the worst, a surge of energy rippled through the air. The hulking man suddenly stopped firing, his grin vanishing as his eyes squeezed shut in pain. A brilliant glow surrounded his head, and the air shimmered with the unmistakable signs of Tether magic.

"Miss me?" Katura's voice called out, light and teasing despite the tension.

Grayson turned his head to see Katura standing on the ridge above, her hands glowing as she manipulated the Tether with practiced ease. The blinding light she'd conjured around the man's face rendered him helpless, his hands clawing at the air as he stumbled back.

A moment later, a massive figure charged onto the scene. Yulen, his huge war hammer held high, roared as he barreled toward the disoriented pirate. With a single powerful swing, he slammed the hammer into the steam pack on the man's back. The impact sent sparks flying, and the pack emitted a high-pitched whine as the pressure inside reached a critical point.

"Yulen, move!" Katura shouted.

The oni didn't hesitate, throwing himself to the side just as the steam pack erupted in a fiery explosion. The blast tore through the pirates, the hulking man and his strange weapon consumed in an instant. The shockwave rattled the mountain, sending debris flying and silencing the deadly rifle for good.

Grayson felt the heat of the explosion even from his position and shielded his face as the air cleared. When he looked up, Yulen was standing amidst the wreckage, dusting himself off as if nothing had happened. Katura descended the ridge, her expression a mix of exasperation and relief.

"Cutting it a little close, aren't you?" Grayson called, his voice strained as he finally pulled himself back onto the path.

Katura smirked, though her eyes flicked to his bloodied shoulder with concern. "You're welcome."

Yulen strode over, his war hammer slung across his back. "I figured I napped enough. Nearly missed all the fun."

"Good timing," Jai said, emerging from his hiding spot with a grin. "I was starting to think we were done for."

Starc nodded, his swords still drawn. "That weapon was... something else. If they've got more of those, we're in trouble."

Grayson grimaced, pressing a hand to his shoulder to stem the bleeding. "Then it's a good thing you showed up when you did." He glanced at Katura and Yulen, his tone grateful. "Thanks. Both of you."

Katura waved him off, her smile returning. "You can reward me later. I have a dress that I've been eyeing."

Grayson couldn't help but chuckle, despite the pain. "Let's move. Reinforcements are on the way, but if Blake's in that cavern, I don't want to give him any more time to disappear."

The team regrouped, their resolve unshaken despite the harrowing encounter. Together, they pressed on, the weight of the battle fueling their determination to finish what they'd started.

The team sat quietly by the campfire outside the cavern, the glow of the flames casting flickering shadows against the jagged rocks. They had set up the camp outside the cavern to make sure no other pirates could sneak out and surprise them, but the pirates did not seem to want to engage them any further. The reinforcements from the *Skyward*

Blade finally arrived with the full might of Rainecourt's military—a mix of soldiers, siege engines, and aerial firepower that had quickly overwhelmed the remaining pirates. The sounds of battle had died down hours ago, replaced by the occasional distant shout of a soldier securing the area.

Grayson poked at the fire with a stick, his injured shoulder hastily bandaged and throbbing under his jacket. Katura was unfortunately too drained to mend it right now, so he'd have to deal with it. His mind churned as he processed the day's events, the steam rifle, and the strange, uneasy feeling that had been building since they first set foot on the mountain.

"They've cleared out the last of the resistance," Starc said, approaching the group with a nod. "The cavern's secure. No sign of Blake, though."

Grayson exhaled, the frustration evident in his features. "Of course he's not here. The man's a ghost."

"But he was here," Katura interjected, her tone sharp as she stood and dusted herself off. "You can feel it in the air. There's something... off about this place."

The team gathered their gear and made their way into the cavern, the glow of magical lamps set up by the military illuminating the stone walls. The space was larger than they'd expected, an open chamber with crude wooden crates and supplies stacked along the edges. But it wasn't the supplies that drew their attention—it was the coffins.

Rows of strange, dark coffins lined the far wall of the cavern, each one intricately marked with glowing green glyphs that pulsed faintly, casting an eerie light across the stone floor. The air around them felt heavy, charged with a dark energy that made the hairs on Grayson's neck stand on end.

"What the hell are these?" Jai asked, his voice unusually subdued.

"Bodies," Starc said grimly, pointing to one of the coffins. Its lid was partially ajar, revealing the pale, lifeless form of a villager inside. "These are the ones they took from the raids."

Grayson approached cautiously, his hand resting on the hilt of his pistol. The glyphs on the coffins seemed alive, the patterns shifting slightly as if in response to their presence. "This isn't just storage," he said. "There's something else going on here."

Katura stepped forward, her eyes narrowing as she studied the glyphs. "Let me take a closer look. Maybe I can figure out what these are."

As she reached out to touch one of the glyphs, the glow intensified, and a wave of nausea seemed to radiate from the coffin. Katura stumbled back, clutching her stomach as her face went pale.

"Katura?" Yulen was at her side in an instant, steadying her as she bent over and retched violently onto the cavern floor.

She wiped her mouth, shaking her head as she leaned on Yulen for support. "It's necromancy," she said weakly, her voice trembling. "And not just any necromancy. This is... powerful. Whoever did this, they're not just dabbling. They're a master."

Grayson frowned, his gaze returning to the glyphs. The weight in the air felt heavier now, oppressive. "Can you make sense of it? Figure out who's behind this?"

Katura shook her head, still catching her breath. "No. Not without risking more than I'm willing to. This is beyond me, Grayson. We need someone with a stronger connection to the Tether to even begin to untangle this."

Grayson's mind immediately went to one person. Someone who had proven herself more attuned to the Tether than anyone he'd ever met. "Amaura," he said aloud, drawing curious looks from the others.

Katura straightened, still leaning on Yulen. "The princess's white-haired friend? You think she can handle this?"

"She's more than capable," Grayson replied firmly. "If anyone can figure this out, it's her."

Starc crossed his arms, skeptical but not dismissive. "Do you think she'll even agree to come here? This isn't exactly her battlefield."

Grayson gave a small, wry smile. "If she's anything like I think she is, she'll want to help. We'll need her if we're going to get to the bottom of this."

Jai nodded, his expression serious. "Then we'd better call her. Because whatever this is, it's bad. And if Blake's behind it, we're going to need every advantage we can get."

Grayson sent word back to Tomas, informing him that they needed to make a trip back to the capital. "Tara's not going to love this," he muttered under his breath, "but we don't have a choice."

As the message went out, the team stood in the cavern, the oppressive energy of the coffins lingering like a storm waiting to break. They had taken the first step, but the true danger was only beginning to reveal itself.

Chapter 12

Amaura stared at her reflection in the small mirror in her academy dormitory, her pale fingers carefully adjusting a loose strand of her silvery-white hair. Her heart fluttered with anticipation. Grayson had summoned her—*Grayson!*—and the message had been urgent. He was back in the capital, and he wanted to see her immediately.

She'd barely been able to contain her excitement as she rifled through her modest wardrobe, finally settling on a deep navy-blue tunic embroidered with subtle silver thread, paired with a flowing skirt that swayed with every step. It wasn't extravagant, but it was the nicest thing she owned, and she wanted to look her best.

As Amaura tied a delicate ribbon into her hair, Tryphena leaned against the doorway, her arms crossed and her expression skeptical. "You've been fussing with your hair for twenty minutes. He's not going to notice."

Amaura flushed, glancing at her sister through the mirror. "I'm not... I'm just trying to look presentable."

Tryphena raised an eyebrow. "Wow! He must be really special if you're going to wear that!"

Amaura turned away from the mirror, smoothing her skirt with nervous hands. "It's not a special occasion. It's... it's Grayson. He hasn't been back in weeks, and—"

"And he probably wants something," Tryphena interrupted, her tone blunt. "Don't get your hopes up too much, Amaura. He's a good man, but men like him don't summon people just to catch up. He needs you for something, and I don't want you getting hurt when that's all this turns out to be."

Amaura hesitated, biting her lip. She wanted to believe Tryphena was wrong, but her sister had always been cautious, her experiences making her wary of trusting others too easily. "I know he probably has a reason," Amaura admitted softly, "but... it doesn't matter. I'm just happy to see him again."

Tryphena sighed, stepping forward to rest a hand on Amaura's shoulder. "I'm not saying don't go. Just... be careful. Don't let that excitement blind you. You've been through too much to get your heart broken now."

Amaura smiled faintly, placing her hand over Tryphena's. "I'll be fine. But thank you."

Tryphena didn't look convinced, but she nodded and stepped back, allowing Amaura to gather her things. As Amaura slipped out the door and made her way toward the meeting point, her heart raced with a mix of nerves and excitement.

Maybe Tryphena was right. Maybe this was just business. But Amaura couldn't shake the hope that, just maybe, Grayson had thought of her as more than just someone useful for whatever task he had in mind. Whatever the reason, she was about to see him again, and that was enough to quicken her pulse and lighten her steps.

Amaura arrived at the meeting point, her heart pounding with a mix of excitement and nervousness. Grayson was waiting for her in a quiet corner of the capital's Sentinel outpost, his posture relaxed but his face etched with weariness. His armor bore fresh scuffs, his jacket slightly torn at the shoulder, and dark circles shadowed his eyes. Yet, when he saw her, he managed a tired but genuine smile.

"Amaura," he said warmly, standing as she approached. "It's good to see you."

"You too," she replied, her cheeks warming slightly under his gaze. She noticed his eyes linger for a moment longer than usual before he tilted his head, his expression curious.

"Did you... do something with your hair?" he asked, a small grin tugging at his lips. "It looks nice."

Amaura's face flushed deeper, and she absently touched the ribbon she'd tied in earlier. "Oh, I—thank you."

Grayson chuckled, his smile fading slightly as he ran a hand through his hair. "I really wish we had time to catch up properly, but I need to get to the point." He gestured for her to sit at the small table nearby, and as she did, his tone turned more serious.

"Do you remember," he began, "when we talked about me recruiting you for the Sentinels after you finished at the Academy?"

She nodded, her heart racing. "Yes, I remember."

"Well…" He sighed, leaning back in his chair. "I might need you a little sooner than that. At least temporarily."

Amaura blinked, taken aback. "You do?"

Grayson nodded, his expression grim. "We've been chasing these pirates for weeks, and we've uncovered something big. They're working with someone capable of incredibly powerful necromancy. We found… coffins, marked with glyphs, tied to the bodies they've been stealing from raids. The Tether energy coming off them is overwhelming—too much for even my team's most skilled mage to handle."

Her stomach twisted at the mention of necromancy, but she sat straighter, listening intently.

"Katura tried to study the glyphs, but it made her sick. We need someone more attuned to the Tether to help us figure out what's going on, someone with your… unique gifts. It's the only way we'll get to the bottom of this."

Amaura's excitement deflated slightly as she realized why he had called her here. *Tryphena was right,* she thought. He needed her help, not her company. But as disappointment flickered, it was quickly overshadowed by a sense of purpose. This was an opportunity—a chance to prove herself to him, to show that she was more than just a student. More than just an Aborrent.

She met his gaze, her own steady. "I'll do it. Whatever you need, I'm in."

Grayson's smile returned, soft and grateful. "I knew I could count on you."

Amaura stood, already mentally preparing herself for the task ahead. "I'll need to gather a few things from the Academy and let my instructors know I'll be gone for a while. When do we leave?"

"As soon as you're ready," Grayson said, standing as well. "This isn't going to be easy, Amaura. But I wouldn't have asked if I didn't think you could handle it."

"I can handle it," she said firmly, a mix of determination and excitement bubbling in her chest. "I won't let you down."

Grayson placed a hand on her shoulder, his touch light but reassuring. "I never thought you would."

As she turned to leave and prepare, her heart raced for an entirely different reason. She wasn't just helping Grayson with a mission; she was stepping into his world, his team, even if only for a short time. The thought of working alongside him, of proving her worth in front of him, filled her with equal parts fear and exhilaration.

Tryphena's words echoed faintly in her mind, but Amaura pushed them aside. For now, all that mattered was the task ahead—and the man who believed in her enough to ask for her help.

Grayson entered the princess's study, his posture rigid but his expression calm, as always. Tara was seated on her usual plush couch, but there was no warmth in her face this time. Her lips were pressed into a tight line, and her fingers drummed nervously against the armrest. She felt tense all of a sudden.

"Grayson," she began, her tone sharper than usual. "I heard about your latest... addition to your mission."

He inclined his head slightly. "You mean Amaura."

"Yes, Amaura." Tara's voice softened as she said the name, though her expression remained stern. "You brought her into this? Into danger?"

Grayson didn't flinch under her gaze. "She's the only one who can help us right now, Tara. We're dealing with powerful necromancy—far beyond what anyone on my team can handle. Amaura's connection to the Tether makes her uniquely suited for this."

"She's also barely more than a student," Tara countered, rising from her seat. "She's been through so much already. She's still adjusting to this new life, to who she is. And now you're dragging her into a battlefield?"

Grayson took a step forward, his voice steady but firm. "I'm not dragging her anywhere. I explained the risks, and she agreed. She wants to help. And I promise you, I will be looking out for her."

Tara's hands balled into fists at her sides. "And what happens when you can't? What happens if something goes wrong, and she—" She cut herself off, her voice catching. "She's been hurt enough, Grayson. I don't want to see her go through anything like that again."

"She won't," Grayson said, his tone resolute. "I'll make sure of it. I'd sacrifice my own life before I let anything happen to her."

The words were barely out of his mouth before Tara's composure broke. "Why?" she snapped, her voice sharp and trembling with emotion. "Why are you so willing to die?"

Grayson blinked, caught off guard by her outburst. "Tara—"

"No," she interrupted, her voice rising. "You act like your life is something you can just throw away! Like it doesn't matter. But it does. It matters to—" She stopped short, clenching her fists as she struggled to keep her emotions in check. "Why don't you care about your own life, Grayson?"

He sighed, his shoulders slumping slightly. "I'm a soldier, Tara. I don't want to die. But I've always known that any mission could be my last. It's part of the job."

"That's not an answer!" she shouted, her voice cracking. "You're not just a soldier. You're—" She faltered again, turning away from him and pressing a hand to her temple. "If you don't care about your own life, then why should I?"

Grayson's jaw tightened, but he remained silent. The weight of her words hung heavy in the air, and for a moment, neither of them spoke.

Finally, Tara turned back to him, her eyes shining with unshed tears. "Just... just don't let anything happen to her. If you care about Amaura even half as much as you claim to, you'll keep her safe. No matter what."

Grayson straightened, nodding solemnly. "I swear to you, Tara. I won't let anything happen to her."

He turned to leave, his boots heavy against the stone floor as he exited the study. The door closed softly behind him, leaving Tara alone with her thoughts.

She sank back onto the couch, her head in her hands. Her chest ached with a mix of guilt and confusion. She didn't understand why she'd snapped at him, why his willingness to sacrifice himself had hit her so hard. He was right—he was a soldier. He'd always known the risks. But something about the way he'd said it, so calm, so matter-of-fact...

Tara wiped her eyes, forcing herself to take a deep breath. She hated how out of control her emotions had felt, how she'd lashed out without thinking. And she hated how much the idea of losing him—losing Grayson—scared her. She didn't know why it did, but the fear was there, buried deep, refusing to let go.

Amaura stepped onto the deck of the *Enduring*, her heart racing as she looked around the airship's interior. It was larger than she had imagined, its polished brass fittings gleaming in the sunlight that poured through the portholes. The hum of its engines vibrated through the floor, a constant reminder of its power and purpose.

She clutched the strap of her satchel tightly, her nerves threatening to get the better of her. This was the first time she'd been among Grayson's team since they had freed her and Tryphena from slavery, and the memories of that time clung to her like a shadow. These people knew the truth about her past—about what she was. She wasn't sure if they would accept her or see her as a burden.

Her thoughts were interrupted by a booming voice.

"Amaura!" Yulen's deep, jovial tone filled the air as he strode forward, his massive frame towering over her. "It's been too long, little mage!" He scooped her up into a bear hug before she could protest, laughing heartily as he set her down. "You've grown stronger, haven't you? I can feel it! I knew you'd become something special."

Amaura blinked, momentarily overwhelmed by his enthusiasm. "I—I've been trying," she stammered, a small smile creeping onto her face despite herself.

Jai leaned casually against the wall nearby, flipping one of his daggers in his hand. "We're counting on you, Amaura," he said with a smirk. "You're the star of this mission. Don't let us down."

Starc, standing next to him, gave her a nod, his expression more serious but no less sincere. "He's right. We wouldn't be bringing you along if we didn't think you could handle this. We need you."

The warmth of their words began to melt her nervousness. "Thank you," she said quietly, her voice steadying. "I'll do my best."

Katura sauntered up, her sharp gaze sweeping over Amaura appraisingly. "Well, look at you," she said with a grin. "Nice hair. I like the ribbon—suits you." She gestured toward one of the seats. "You know, I've got a few tricks for styling hair during long flights. Stick with me, and we'll have you looking like royalty by the time we land."

Amaura flushed, caught between embarrassment and gratitude. "That's... kind of you," she said softly.

Tomas cleared his throat, stepping forward with a book in hand. "As much as Katura might want to play stylist," he said with a faint smile, "we have more pressing matters. Amaura, we'll need to use this flight to give you a primer on the Tether of the Plane of Death. It's the source of necromantic power, and while Katura and I aren't experts, we can give you enough of an understanding to get started."

Amaura nodded, straightening her posture. "Of course. I'm ready to learn."

"Good," Tomas said, his tone encouraging. "The more you know, the better prepared you'll be when we reach the site."

Katura leaned in, lowering her voice just enough for Amaura to hear. "Don't let him scare you with all the talk of death planes and necromancy. You've already got a strong connection to the Tether. This will just be another layer."

Amaura smiled, her confidence growing as she looked around at the group. She had been so worried about how they would react to her presence, but instead of judgment or wariness, she found herself greeted with camaraderie and support. These weren't just Grayson's allies—they were her allies now, too.

For the first time in a long while, Amaura felt like she belonged.

The air in the cavern was oppressive, heavy with the unnatural energy radiating from the coffins. The glyphs etched into their surfaces pulsed faintly, their sickly green light casting eerie shadows across the stone walls. Amaura stood before them, her hands trembling slightly as she prepared to tap into the Tether of the Plane of Death. The military guards flanked the room, their expressions wary and tense, though none dared approach the coffins. They had strict orders not to touch them, and their unease was palpable.

Grayson stood nearby, his gaze steady as he watched her. "You've got this," he said, his voice calm and reassuring. "We're right here if you need us."

Amaura nodded, though her heart was pounding. She could feel the weight of their expectations, the knowledge that they were counting on her to uncover the secrets of these macabre artifacts. Taking a deep breath, she extended her hands toward the nearest coffin, her fingers brushing the cold, rough surface. She closed her eyes and reached out with her mind, tapping into the Tether that wove through the glyphs.

The sensation was immediate and revolting. It felt like plunging into freezing, stagnant water filled with writhing worms that crawled across her skin. The sickly power clung to her, seeping into her very being, and she shivered as a wave of nausea rolled over her. But she didn't stop. She couldn't.

The energy surrounding the coffins became clearer in her mind, its patterns unraveling as she pushed deeper into the connection. She could see the glyphs channeling the power of death, funneling it into the corpses inside. The bodies were changing, their forms being twisted and altered by the necromantic energy. They were being prepared for... something. But that wasn't all. The power didn't stop there—it stretched beyond the coffins, branching outward like tendrils, carrying its influence somewhere distant. Someone—or something—was observing them.

A sudden jolt of awareness struck Amaura like a physical blow, and an image appeared in her mind. It was a man, or what had once been a man. His flesh was rotted, mummified, as though death had claimed him but refused to finish the job. Goggles, seemingly fused into his decayed face, glowed with a sickly green light that pulsed with unnatural energy. The man's gaze locked onto her, and though it was just an image in her mind, Amaura felt his attention like an icy hand gripping her throat.

"Interesting," the man's voice rasped, echoing through her thoughts. It was dry and cracked, like the sound of old paper tearing. "Such promise. Such untapped potential. A fountain of power, waiting to be shaped. Simply amazing and pleasantly unexpected."

Amaura froze, her breathing shallow as the man continued. External interference in my endeavors is... His tone shifted, almost reverent. "You, I will make an exception for. There is greatness in you, child. A spark waiting to ignite."

She tried to pull back, but the image held her fast. His attention was unrelenting, as though he could see through her, into the very depths of her soul.

"I conduct my research in a tower," the man said, his tone almost conversational. "An abandoned monument of stone and ruin, where death dances freely. Come to me, little spark. Let us see where your promise leads."

The image faded as suddenly as it had appeared, leaving Amaura gasping for air. She stumbled back from the coffin, her legs weak and trembling. Grayson was at her side in an instant, steadying her with a firm hand on her arm.

"Amaura! Are you alright?" he asked, his voice laced with concern.

She nodded, though her face was pale, and her eyes were wide. "I... I saw him," she whispered. "The one behind this. He spoke to me."

Grayson's brow furrowed. "Spoke to you? What did he say?"

Amaura swallowed hard, her throat dry. "He's... experimenting. These coffins, the glyphs, they're part of his research. He called me... interesting. Said I have potential. And then..." She hesitated, glancing around at the others. "He told me where to find him. An abandoned tower, ruins to the north. He... he wants me to go there."

Grayson went silent, his eyes wide. He wasn't the kind of person to be surprised easily, but this had caught even him off guard.

The faint sound of shifting metal broke the tense silence in the cavern, and Amaura turned toward the nearest coffin just in time to see its lid slide open with a low, ominous creak. Her heart stopped as the corpse inside, its flesh pale and mottled with decay, began to rise. The glyphs on the coffin pulsed with an eerie green light, as if feeding the thing with power, and its sunken eyes locked onto her with a hunger that made her blood run cold.

Before Amaura could react, the undead lunged at her, its teeth bared and its skeletal fingers reaching for her throat. She froze, paralyzed by terror, her mind screaming for her to move, but her body refused to obey.

"Amaura!" Grayson's voice rang out like a thunderclap.

In an instant, he was between her and the creature. His sword flashed in the dim light, and with a single, decisive swing, the corpse's head was severed from its body. The head hit the ground with a sickening thud, rolling to a stop, while the decapitated body crumpled lifelessly at his feet.

Amaura stumbled back, her breathing ragged, as Grayson turned to her, his voice urgent. "Are you alright?"

Before she could answer, another creak echoed through the cavern, then another. The lids of the other coffins were beginning to shift, the glyphs flaring brightly as the undead within began to stir. One by one, they emerged, their movements jerky and unnatural, their rotting forms emitting guttural growls that sent shivers down Amaura's spine.

The soldiers stationed around the cavern shouted warnings, raising their weapons as the undead charged. The air erupted into chaos as the creatures lunged at the living, their teeth and claws tearing through flesh and armor. Screams of pain and the sickening crunch of bones filled the air as some of the soldiers fell, their blood pooling on the cavern floor.

"Fall back!" Grayson roared, his voice cutting through the din. "Everyone, retreat! Now!"

The soldiers began to pull back, firing shots at the advancing undead as they scrambled toward the cavern entrance. Grayson grabbed Amaura's arm, pulling her along with him as the undead surged forward. Starc and Jai flanked them, their weapons cutting down any creature that got too close, but the sheer number of the undead threatened to overwhelm them.

As they neared the cavern entrance, Amaura stopped suddenly, wrenching her arm free from Grayson's grip. "Keep going!" she shouted, turning back to face the horde.

"Amaura, what are you doing?!" Grayson yelled, his voice filled with alarm.

She didn't answer. Closing her eyes, she reached deep into the Tether, summoning the raw, burning power that had lain dormant within her for so long. The energy surged through her, fiery and unrelenting, and she raised her hands toward the cavern.

The air around her crackled with heat as flames erupted from her fingertips, racing into the cavern like a living force. The fire roared as it consumed everything in its path, engulfing the coffins, the glyphs, and the undead in a blazing inferno. The heat was intense, searing the air, and the guttural growls of the undead turned to shrieks of agony as the flames consumed them.

Grayson shielded his face from the heat, his eyes wide as he watched the cavern burn. The firelight danced across Amaura's face, her expression a mix of focus and fury as she poured her power into the flames.

Finally, the flames began to die down, leaving nothing but smoldering ashes and the charred remains of the undead. Amaura lowered her hands, her body trembling with exhaustion as the last embers faded.

Grayson approached her cautiously, his sword still in hand. "Amaura..." he began, his voice softer now. "Are you okay?"

She turned to him, her face pale and her breathing uneven, but her eyes were resolute. "I'm fine," she said, though her voice trembled slightly. "It's done. They're gone."

Grayson glanced back at the soldiers, some of whom were nursing injuries, their faces a collage of relief and fear. He turned back to Amaura, placing a steadying hand on her shoulder. "You saved us."

Amaura looked away, unsure how to respond. The memory of the necromancer's words still echoed in her mind, and the sensation of the Tether of Death still clung to her like a shadow. But for now, she pushed those thoughts aside. They had survived. That was what mattered.

Chapter 13

Grayson leaned against a craggy boulder just outside the tower, his pistol holstered but his hand never far from it. They arrived after dusk as the dark silhouette of the abandoned structure loomed against the dark, twin moon-lit sky, its crooked spire reaching like a skeletal finger into the heavens. The air was thick with tension, the kind that made the hair on the back of his neck stand on end.

This mission unsettled him in a way few others did. He'd fought men, monsters, and the chaos they wrought, but this—this was something else. The necromancer they were hunting, this melding of human cunning and monstrous magic, was a danger far greater than anything he was used to. It wasn't just a fight for survival—it was a fight against the unknown, and that always made him uneasy.

Grayson turned his gaze toward the soldiers standing at attention nearby, their expressions resolute. A small military escort had accompanied his team, ready to raid the tower at his signal. He wasn't used to commanding more than his own team; the added responsibility of so many lives weighed heavily on his shoulders. But if the tower housed more undead or a contingent of pirates, the reinforcements would be necessary.

The faint sound of movement brought his attention to the shadowy edge of the forest. A moment later, Jai emerged, moving with the practiced ease of a predator. He approached Grayson and the others, his expression serious.

"What did you see?" Grayson asked, straightening.

Jai shook his head, sheathing his daggers. "More coffins. Same design as the ones back at the pirate hideout. But they're all empty."

"Empty?" Amaura stepped forward, her brow furrowing.

"Yeah," Jai confirmed. "No bodies, no glyphs, nothing. If there were any undead or pirates here, they're long gone. The place feels abandoned."

Grayson frowned, his unease deepening. An empty tower wasn't what he'd expected. "No sign of the necromancer?"

"Not a trace," Jai replied. "If he's here, he's doing a damn good job hiding."

Grayson's jaw tightened as he turned his gaze back to the tower. "Then we go in and conduct a thorough investigation. If there's anything to find, we'll find it."

He turned to the military officers waiting nearby. "Stay on standby. If you hear the signal, move in immediately. Tomas, you're staying out here to coordinate with them."

Tomas raised an eyebrow. "You sure about that? You might need my support inside on this one."

"I'm sure," Grayson said firmly. "If things go south, I need someone out here who can hold the line and get those soldiers moving. That's you."

Tomas nodded reluctantly, stepping back toward the officers as Grayson gestured to the rest of the team.

"Let's move," he said, his voice steady.

Amaura followed close behind, her nerves visible. Starc and Katura flanked her, while Yulen brought up the rear, his massive war hammer slung across his back. Jai stayed ahead, his movements silent as he led them toward the tower.

As they approached the entrance, Grayson cast one last glance at the soldiers waiting in the shadows. The weight of their lives pressed against him, but he pushed the thought aside. For now, his focus had to be on the team and the task at hand.

The heavy wooden door of the tower creaked as Grayson pushed it open, the sound echoing into the dark interior. The air inside was stale, heavy with the scent of mildew and something else—a faint, metallic tang that set his teeth on edge.

"Stay sharp," he said quietly, his voice barely more than a whisper. "Whatever's in here, it's not going to give us a warm welcome."

With that, they stepped inside, their footsteps muffled by the thick layer of dust that covered the stone floor. The dim light of their lanterns cast long, flickering shadows on the walls as they began their search, the oppressive silence of the tower pressing down on them like a weight.

The stench inside the tower was nearly unbearable, a rancid mix of decay, mildew, and something sickly sweet that clung to the back of Grayson's throat. The dim lantern light revealed a grim tableau: rows of coffins stacked haphazardly against the walls, their lids askew as though their contents had been disturbed; bookshelves groaning under the weight of ancient tomes whose spines were cracked and blackened with age; and tables strewn with bizarre instruments—bladed tools, glass containers filled with viscous fluids, and strange, rune-etched contraptions that defied explanation.

Grayson grimaced, his hand resting on the hilt of his sword as he surveyed the unsettling scene. "This place is a tomb of madness," he muttered, his voice low but carrying an edge of tension.

Katura, standing near one of the tables, shivered visibly. "I don't like this," she said, her usual smirk replaced by a rare seriousness. "The energy here are all wrong. We should leave."

"We'll leave soon enough," Grayson replied, his tone steady. "But we need answers first. Just bear with it a little longer."

Amaura moved cautiously through the room, her hands outstretched as she reached for the invisible threads of the Tether. Her face was pale, her brow furrowed in concentration. "The Tether of Death is strong here," she said softly, her voice barely above a whisper. "It's everywhere, woven into the walls, the air... but I can't pinpoint its source."

As they continued their search, Grayson suddenly heard Tomas's voice. "Grayson! We've got a problem—big one."

Grayson's chest tightened at the urgency in Tomas's tone. "What's happening?"

"Undead," Tomas replied, his words coming in bursts over the sound of chaos. "They just... sprung up from the ground. Dozens—no, hundreds—of them. They're all over the camp!"

Grayson's eyes narrowed, his grip tightening on his pistol. "Get the ships ready to take off! Don't stand and fight, just retreat!"

Tomas's reply came, but it was interrupted by a sharp, agonized yell that pierced through Grayson's mind like a blade and he jolted, nearly dropping his weapon.

"Tomas!" he shouted, his voice echoing through the tower. "Tomas, respond!"

There was no reply—only static and the distant, faint sounds of battle.

Grayson turned to the team, his face grim. "We're leaving. Now. Get ready to fight our way through."

Before anyone could respond, the floor beneath them shuddered violently, the stones groaning as if alive. Grayson's instincts flared, and he barked, "Watch the—"

But it was too late. The floor gave way with a deafening crack, the stones crumbling beneath their feet as the entire room collapsed into a dark, yawning void.

Amaura screamed as she fell, the dim light from their lanterns swallowed by the blackness. Grayson reached out, trying to grab hold of anything to stop his descent, but his fingers found only air. The team's voices were lost in the chaos as they plummeted into the unknown, the oppressive darkness swallowing them whole.

The last thing Grayson saw before the void consumed him was the faint, sickly glow of glyphs etched into the crumbling walls, pulsing like a heartbeat. A blinding burst of light, then—nothing.

Amaura awoke on cold, damp stone, the sensation sending a shiver up her spine. She blinked rapidly, her vision adjusting to the dim, sickly light that surrounded her. The air was thick with an unnatural stillness, the oppressive weight of something ancient and malevolent pressing down on her chest. Slowly, she pushed herself up, her eyes widening as she took in her surroundings.

She was on an island—a jagged piece of land jutting out in the middle of a river that pulsed and glowed with an eerie green light. The river wasn't water. It was Tether, pure and unfiltered, flowing with the energy of the Plane of Death itself. Her breath caught in her throat at the sight. How was this possible? Could they have fallen into the plane itself?

Then she saw it. She took it at first as a waterfall, but it was more of a fountain, spewing the Tether up into the air before it came crashing down to join the river. At the base of the fountain was something she had seen in many books at the Academy but had never witnessed in person: an obelisk. A font of Tether directly connected to the plane of its source, second in power only to the primordial monoliths. It didn't take a stretch of the imagination to know this obelisk was connected to the Plane of Death. But how did such a rare and powerful artifact find its way here?

As the questions swirled in her mind, she spotted her companions. Grayson, Katura, Yulen, Jai, and Starc were all bound in chains of crackling green energy, their forms slumped and their weapons discarded. Their usual strength and defiance were gone, replaced by grimaces of pain and exhaustion. Amaura's heart sank at the sight, her instinct to help them warring with her rising panic.

"Ah, you're awake. I trust my teleportation trap did not... damage you."

The voice was dry and hollow, like the rasp of wind through dead leaves. Amaura turned sharply, and there he was—the rotting man from her vision. He stood tall, his decayed form draped in tattered robes that seemed to pulse faintly with the same sickly green light as the river. The goggles embedded in his mummified face glowed, their unearthly light casting grotesque shadows across his withered features.

"You," Amaura said, her voice steady despite the fear clawing at her chest. "Who are you? What do you want?"

The man inclined his head slightly, his movements deliberate, almost reverent. "I am whom I have always been," he said, his tone both regal and condescending. "My mortal name has long since lost its meaning. It is irrelevant to what I have become, the power I now hold as a lich."

Amaura's fists clenched at her sides. "What do you want from us?"

The lich's gaze lingered on her, his glowing eyes seeming to pierce straight through her. "Ah, child," he said softly, as though speaking to a curious pupil. "All I have ever wanted is to be left in peace to conduct my research, to unravel the mysteries of life and death. But alas, the world has a way of interfering with one's pursuits. This gift practically fell into my lap." He gestured to her with a skeletal hand. "You may be the key I have been waiting for all this time."

Amaura stiffened. "What do you mean?"

The lich stepped closer, his movements slow and deliberate, like a predator savoring its prey. "You are unique," he said, his voice low and filled with dark fascination. "Not quite living, not quite dead. Not quite human, not quite beast. Connected to the Tether in ways no other soul I have encountered could hope to be. You are a perfect conduit for the Tether of Death—untethered, bound to no single plane. You are power incarnate, child, and I will use you. You are... a Savant!"

The words sent a chill through her, but they also ignited a spark of defiance in her chest. "No," she said firmly, her voice cutting through the oppressive air. She stepped forward, raising her hands as she prepared to channel the Tether. "I won't be used."

The lich raised a hand before she could act. Instantly, her companions screamed in unison, their bodies writhing as the chains binding them flared with purple energy. The sound tore through the air like jagged glass, and Amaura froze, horror flashing across her face.

"Do not be so hasty," the lich said, his tone calm but carrying an undeniable edge of menace. "You may refuse me, but it is they who will pay the price for your defiance. Consider your choices carefully, child."

Amaura's hands trembled, the power she had begun to summon dissipating as her gaze flicked between the lich and her companions. Grayson's jaw was clenched in agony, his eyes locked on hers even through the pain, as though willing her not to give in. But the others—Jai, Starc, Yulen, and Katura—they were breaking under the strain, their screams growing weaker, more desperate.

"Please," she whispered, her voice shaking. "Let them go."

The lich tilted his head, almost mockingly. "Their fate lies in your hands, child. Accept your role, and they may yet live. Refuse... and they will suffer until the very end."

Amaura's mind raced, torn between the unbearable thought of letting him use her and the sight of her friends in torment. The green river pulsed around them, a dark and relentless rhythm, as the lich waited for her decision.

Amaura stood frozen, her eyes darting between her companions and the lich. Grayson's eyes gave her a desperate plea: *Don't listen to him.* But the sight of the chains wracking her friends with pain—Grayson included—left her no choice. Her heart ached, but her resolve hardened. If this was the only way to save them, she would do it.

Slowly, she raised her chin and met the lich's glowing gaze. "What do you want me to do?" she asked, her voice trembling but steady.

The lich's rotted face stretched into a grotesque imitation of a smile as he reached into the folds of his tattered robe and pulled out a stone. It was dark and smooth, pulsing faintly with a deep, green light. At its center, a glowing glyph in the shape of a key shifted and twisted as though alive.

"Take this," he said, holding the stone out to her. "Hold it close to your chest, and then step into the river. Submerge yourself fully in the Tether."

Amaura recoiled instinctively at the thought. The river pulsed with raw, unfiltered energy from the Plane of Death, a power so unnatural and foul that even standing near it made her skin crawl. Submerging herself in it felt like a death sentence—or worse.

She swallowed hard, steeling herself. "If I do this, you have to let them go," she warned, her voice firm. "All of them. No harm. They walk free when this is done."

The lich tilted his head, his expression unreadable behind the green glow of his embedded goggles. "When this is done," he said, his voice eerily calm, "I will have no use for them. They will be free to go as they wish."

"Amaura, don't!" Grayson's voice rang out, desperate and furious. "You don't know what he's doing! Don't trust him—"

His words turned into a pained yell as the chains around him flared, sending visible arcs of energy through his body. He collapsed to his knees, his face twisted in agony.

"Grayson!" Amaura's heart wrenched at the sight, tears springing to her eyes. Seeing him like this, broken and helpless, filled her with a new kind of resolve. She couldn't bear to see him suffer—not him, not the others. She clenched her fists, drawing strength from the depth of her feelings. *Anything for him.*

"I'll do it," she said, her voice shaking but resolute. She stepped forward and took the stone from the lich's skeletal hand. The moment her fingers closed around it, an icy chill seeped into her palm, spreading like a web through her veins.

"Good," the lich said, his tone almost reverent. "Now, step into the river."

Amaura turned toward the glowing green current, her grip tightening on the stone as her stomach churned. Each step toward the edge felt heavier than the last, the pulsing energy of the Tether growing stronger, its presence invasive and suffocating.

She paused at the bank, the stone pressed tightly to her chest. "You promise," she said, her voice barely above a whisper, though it was laced with defiance. "You promise you'll let them go."

The lich nodded, his gaze unyielding. "They will walk free."

Amaura closed her eyes and stepped into the river.

The moment her foot touched the glowing surface, icy tendrils coiled around her ankle, dragging her deeper. She gasped, the cold biting through her flesh as she waded further in, the water—or whatever it was—rising around her legs, her waist, her chest. The stone in her hand grew hotter, pulsing with the same rhythm as the Tether surrounding her.

Then, she submerged herself completely.

The sensation was immediate and horrifying. It was as though worms made of ice burrowed under her skin, slithering into her blood and racing toward her heart. They coiled around her bones, her organs, her mind. Her body convulsed as the power of the Tether overwhelmed her, flooding her senses with darkness and death. She tried to scream, but no sound escaped her lips. The river's energy filled her throat, her lungs, choking her cries into silence.

She felt as though she were dissolving, her body breaking apart and becoming one with the Tether. Visions flickered in her mind—ghostly shapes, decayed landscapes, endless voids filled with writhing shadows. Through it all, the lich's voice echoed faintly in her thoughts, low and triumphant.

"Do not fear, child. You are becoming something greater."

Amaura's mind spiraled as the void threatened to consume her, and in her final moment of clarity, she thought of Grayson. His voice, his presence, his determination. *I have to hold on. For him. For all of them.*

And then, she was gone, swallowed entirely by the river.

Grayson's heart clenched as he watched Amaura disappear beneath the glowing green surface of the Tether river. The unnatural light pulsed rhythmically, mocking him with its alien calmness. He clenched his fists, helpless to do anything as the lich loomed nearby, his grotesque figure exuding an air of smug patience.

"We have to do something," Grayson muttered, his voice a mix of despair and fury.

Katura, still bound in the crackling purple chains, whispered beside him, her voice strained. "I'm almost there. Just a little more time."

Grayson turned to her, his sharp eyes catching the beads of sweat rolling down her face. He realized how much effort it must have taken for her to push against the lich's Tether this whole time, her own Tether straining to find the weak points in their bindings. He nodded, silently signaling his trust in her, and cast a glance at where their weapons had fallen when they'd been captured.

With a subtle nod, Grayson signaled the others. Yulen, Jai, and Starc, bound but ready, understood immediately, their tense postures shifting as they prepared to act.

"This space, Grayson," Katura whispered through labored breaths, "I can't be sure, but I believe that man has somehow created a space that mirrors the Plane of Death using its very Tether. If that is true, we'll be fighting against him in his own domain, where he will have complete control. I don't know if we can win."

"What other choice do we have?" Grayson whispered back.

She nodded. A low growl escaped Katura's lips as she pushed one last time. "Get ready," she whispered. Then, with a flash of energy, the chains burst apart, releasing them all in an explosion of violet light.

Grayson moved instantly, diving for his sword and pistol. He grabbed the pistol first and fired a shot directly at the lich. The bullet struck true, but the necromancer merely turned his head, the projectile disintegrating into harmless sparks against a shimmering barrier of energy.

Grayson gritted his teeth, switching to his sword. He charged forward, swinging the blade in a wide arc, but a wave of sickly green energy radiated from the lich, slamming into him like a tidal wave and sending him flying backward. He crashed to the ground with a grunt, his sword clattering from his grip.

Yulen roared, hefting his massive war hammer as he barreled toward the lich. The oni's strength was unmatched, and his swing connected with a thunderous impact, sending the rotted necromancer sprawling to the ground. The lich snarled, his glowing eyes flaring with rage.

"Go!" Yulen bellowed, his voice booming like thunder. "Save Amaura! We'll handle this!"

Grayson didn't hesitate. Scrambling to his feet, he sprinted toward the river, its unnatural glow casting an otherworldly light across his face. The lich's voice rose in a furious roar behind him.

"Stop!" the necromancer bellowed, his voice reverberating with power. "The girl is only half-finished! You'll ruin everything!"

Ignoring the warning, Grayson kneeled at the edge of the river and plunged his hand into the Tether.

The cold was immediate and excruciating, numbing his arm as if the blood in his veins had turned to ice. It was unlike anything he'd ever felt, a biting chill that radiated through his entire body. His fingers searched desperately through the writhing energy, his teeth clenched against the pain.

"Come on," he muttered through gritted teeth. "Come on, Amaura!"

His hand brushed against something, and he grabbed it—a hand, slender and lifeless. Summoning every ounce of his strength, Grayson pulled, the numbing cold creeping up his arm as if the river itself was trying to claim him. With a final, desperate heave, he yanked Amaura from the Tether.

Her body was limp, her skin pale and marked with black, spidery veins that ran up her arms and crept across her face. Grayson's heart sank as he kneeled over her, fearing the worst. "Amaura!" he shouted, shaking her gently. He knocked the stone from her hands. It left part of its glyph on her hand and sizzled on the ground where it landed. "Amaura, wake up!"

For a terrifying moment, there was no response. Then she coughed violently, her chest heaving as she gasped for air. Grayson exhaled in relief, his shoulders sagging as he cradled her against him.

"You're okay," he murmured, his voice soft. "You're okay."

It was only then that he noticed his own hand. The flesh was shriveled and blackened, the veins dark and sunken as though decayed by the river's touch. He flexed his fingers experimentally, feeling a dull ache but no loss of movement. There was no time to dwell on it.

The lich's roar of rage filled the air, shaking the ground beneath them. "You insolent worms!" he bellowed, rising to his feet as sickly green energy crackled around him. "You could have walked away with your lives! But now you will die a thousand deaths!"

The ground around the island began to quake as more tendrils of Tether rose from the river, twisting and writhing like serpents preparing to strike. Grayson clutched Amaura tightly, his jaw set as he turned to the others, who had regrouped and were standing firm against the lich.

"Hold strong!" he shouted, his voice carrying over the chaos. "We're not letting this bastard win!"

The battle was far from over, but Grayson's resolve burned brighter than ever. They had saved Amaura, and now they would finish what they had started—no matter the cost.

Chapter 14

The air was thick with the acrid smell of burnt ozone and decayed flesh as Grayson's team fought desperately against the lich. The necromancer stood in the center of the chaos, his tattered robes billowing as though caught in an invisible storm, the sickly green glow of his embedded goggles illuminating his grotesque, mummified face. His every movement radiated power, and the ground beneath him pulsed with the energy of the Plane of Death.

Starc lunged forward, his twin swords flashing in the dim light as he struck at the lich with all his might. The blades connected with the necromancer's barrier, but instead of slicing through, they skittered off harmlessly, sparks flying as if they had hit solid steel. Starc snarled in frustration, stepping back to avoid a retaliatory strike.

Jai slipped into the shadows, his form disappearing in a blur of movement as he circled behind the lich. His daggers glinted as he struck, aiming for the vulnerable spot between the lich's shoulder blades. But the necromancer's barrier flared, repelling the blades with a sharp burst of energy that sent Jai stumbling back.

Yulen roared, hefting his war hammer once more. The oni's sheer strength and size made him a force to be reckoned with, and his swing was powerful enough to shatter stone. But as the hammer descended, a tendril of sickly green energy shot out from the lich's barrier, wrapping around Yulen's waist and lifting him into the air. He thrashed, growling and straining against the tendril's unyielding grip.

Grayson gritted his teeth, gripping his pistol tightly. His left hand throbbed with dull pain, the decayed skin reminding him of what was at stake. Activating the lightning charge on his pistol, he took careful aim and fired two quick shots at the lich.

The first bolt struck the barrier, exploding in a shower of sparks that briefly disrupted the protective energy. The second shot pierced through, striking the lich in the chest. The necromancer convulsed as electricity coursed through his body, his skeletal frame jerking violently.

"Now!" Grayson shouted.

Seizing the opening, Starc leapt forward, driving both his swords into the lich's chest. The blades sank deep, and for a moment, it seemed as though they had finally gained the upper hand. But the lich's grotesque smile returned, and he moved with unsettling speed, wrapping his bony arms around Starc.

The lyrian cried out, his voice raw with pain, as his body began to wither. His once-proud wings, adorned with vibrant feathers, lost their luster and shed their plumage, leaving only bare, skeletal frames. His skin greyed and cracked as the lich drained the life from him. When the necromancer released him, Starc's lifeless body crumpled to the ground, his once-vibrant presence extinguished.

"No!" Jai's voice was filled with rage as he lunged at the lich, pouncing on him with the fury of a wild animal. His daggers flashed as he stabbed repeatedly at the necromancer's face and neck, his strikes fueled by raw emotion. But before he could do any real damage, another tendril of energy lashed out, coiling around Jai and ripping him away.

Grayson's jaw tightened as he steadied his aim, activating the lightning charge again. He fired directly at the lich's head, but the necromancer raised a hand, deflecting the shot with a wave of energy that sent it ricocheting into the ground. Sparks flew, but the lich remained unharmed, his grotesque grin unwavering.

"Katura!" Grayson yelled, his voice strained.

She didn't hesitate. Reaching deep into the Tether, she sent a surge of violet energy toward the tendrils holding Yulen and Jai. The bindings cracked and shattered under the force of her magic, and the two dropped heavily to the ground. Yulen groaned, rolling to his feet, while Jai scrambled to his knees, his breath ragged and his face twisted with grief and rage.

The remaining team regrouped around Grayson, their movements slower, more deliberate now. They were battered, bloodied, and heartsick over Starc's death. The lich stood tall, his barrier flickering briefly before stabilizing, the glowing glyphs etched into his body pulsating ominously. Despite everything they had thrown at him, he didn't even look injured.

"This isn't working," Katura said, her voice low and grim. Sweat dripped from her temple as she readied herself for whatever came next.

Grayson scanned the battlefield, his mind racing. They had tried everything—steel, magic, brute strength—and none of it had left so much as a scratch. Starc was gone, and the rest of them were running out of options.

But Grayson refused to give up. They hadn't come this far to die here. Not like this. "There's a way to beat him," he said, his voice firm despite the uncertainty gnawing at him. "We just have to find it."

Amaura's eyes fluttered open, and once again, she found herself on the strange island in the middle of the glowing green Tether river. But something was different this time. Her entire body thrummed with an unfamiliar power, a cold and invasive energy that coursed through her veins like icy fire. It wasn't like the Tether she had known all her life—warm, lively, and familiar. This was its opposite: dark, sickly, and all-encompassing, but immense in its grandeur.

She sat up, her senses heightened. The sounds of battle reached her ears—clashes of steel, bursts of magical energy, and the roars of her companions. Her gaze shifted, and she saw them: Grayson and the others, fighting desperately against the lich. Her heart clenched as she saw Grayson on the defensive, a massive tendril of green energy slithering toward him, ready to strike.

Without hesitating, Amaura focused her thoughts, reaching out with the new power coursing through her. The tendril shattered into nothingness, dissolving as if it had never existed. The suddenness of the act left her breathless, but her shock was mirrored by the lich, who turned toward her, his glowing goggles flaring brighter.

"You," the lich hissed, his voice laced with disbelief and anger. Recovering his composure, a distorted smile appeared as he briefly allowed his imagination to run wild with the thought of that power under his control.

Amaura rose to her feet, realization dawning. She could feel the Tether he wielded, the same cold, invasive energy that now coursed through her. But she could do more than feel it—she could control it. It was as if she were tapping into a vast, limitless well, and the lich was merely a part of it.

"You're drawing from the same Tether," Amaura said, her voice steady as she took a step forward. "And I can take it from you."

The lich's barrier pulsed, and more tendrils shot toward her, but with a flick of her wrist, they disintegrated into green mist. The necromancer's skeletal form visibly flinched, and his grotesque smile faltered.

"No," the lich snarled. "You are not ready! You don't understand the power you wield!"

Amaura ignored his words, her focus unwavering as she reached deeper into the Tether. Piece by piece, she stripped the energy from him, starting with his tendrils, then moving to the shimmering barrier that had deflected every attack from her team. It flickered and failed, leaving the lich exposed.

"This wasn't my plan!" the lich said, his voice desperate now. "I have things in motion you can't possibly understand. But I can show you. If you let me help you, I can—"

"No," Amaura interrupted, her voice cold as the power she wielded. "You've hurt too many people. I'm ending this."

She reached out with her mind, pulling the Tether energy from the lich's very being. His skeletal form convulsed, cracks forming across his withered body as the green light in his goggles began to fade.

"Stop!" he screamed, his voice echoing with fury and fear. "You fool! I'll be back and I WILL have your power!"

But Amaura didn't stop. With one final surge of power, she stripped the last vestiges of the Tether from him. His body crumbled into dust, collapsing into a lifeless heap as the green energy dissipated into the void.

There was a blinding flash, and suddenly, the island, the river, and the strange plane of existence were gone. The team found themselves back in the tower, the air heavy with the aftermath of the battle. The lich's body was nowhere to be seen. Amaura fell to the ground exhausted, as though every last bit of energy she had was used up.

Grayson staggered, his face pale and his arm steaming with a sickly green light. The decay from the Tether river had spread further, creeping up his shoulder. He managed a weak smile. "Good work," he said hoarsely, before collapsing to the ground.

"Grayson!" Amaura cried, rushing to his side. She knelt beside him, her hands hovering uncertainly over his arm. The blackened veins and steaming flesh made her stomach churn.

Yulen stepped forward, his massive frame casting a long shadow over them. "We need to get him back to the ship. Quickly," he said, his tone urgent but steady. "Whatever that is, it's killing him." Amaura tried to focus, tried to help him, but all she could manage in her current state of exhaustion was to stop the spreading.

Amaura nodded, determination setting in. She wouldn't let Grayson die—not after everything they had been through.

Grayson's eyes slowly opened, the grogginess in his head making it difficult to focus. The sterile smell of a hospital room filled his senses, and the soft glow of sunlight filtered through a nearby window. His body felt heavy, his movements sluggish as he tried to sit up. Pain flared briefly, dull and distant, as though muted by whatever concoction the healers had given him.

"Take it easy," came a familiar voice, soft but firm.

He turned his head and blinked in surprise. Tara sat beside his bed, her hands folded neatly in her lap, her royal attire conspicuously absent. Instead, she wore a simple, comfortable tunic and trousers, a stark contrast to the composed and regal image she usually projected.

"Princess," he said hoarsely, his throat dry. "Hey, you." He painfully managed a smile.

Tara's lips quirked into a faint smile, though her eyes betrayed a mix of exhaustion and concern. "This is part of my duties," she said evenly. "And I felt it only right that I be here when you woke up. Someone has to take responsibility for the decision I made."

Grayson frowned, confusion flickering across his face. "What decision?"

Tara's smile faded, replaced by a somber expression. She gestured toward his right side. Grayson followed her gaze, his heart sinking as he realized what she was referring to. His arm—his sword arm—was gone. The sleeve of his hospital gown hung limp where the limb had once been.

"The corruption from the Tether was decaying your arm," Tara explained quietly. "No one knew how to stop it. It was killing you. I made the call to have it amputated. It saved your life, but..." She trailed off, her voice heavy with guilt. "I know it's a decision you might not have approved of."

Grayson stared at the empty space for a long moment, the weight of her words settling over him. Finally, he turned back to her, his expression calm despite the turmoil he felt. "Better to be alive with one arm than buried with two," he said, his voice steady. "Thank you for making the call."

Relief flickered in Tara's eyes, though it was quickly tempered by resolve. "I've already ensured our best craftsmen are working on a replacement," she said. "You're far too young to retire from the Sentinels."

Grayson chuckled weakly, though the humor didn't reach his eyes. "You think a new arm will keep me out of trouble?"

"Hardly," Tara said, her smile returning faintly. "But it'll give you one less excuse to sit idle."

Grayson nodded, the gravity of the situation beginning to sink in. "More than my own safety, though... what about the people under my command? The ones I was responsible for. What happened to them?"

Tara's expression darkened, and she hesitated before answering. "Starc and Tomas didn't make it. Neither did a good portion of the military escort. The undead were overwhelming, and... if the lich's defeat hadn't caused them all to crumble, the losses could have been much worse."

Grayson's chest tightened at the news. Starc's vibrant energy, Tomas's steadfast dedication—they were gone. He swallowed hard, his gaze dropping to the bed. "And Amaura?"

"She's recovering," Tara said softly. "The healers say she's physically fine, though they're keeping an eye on her. What she went through..." She paused, her voice faltering slightly. "It would break most people. But she's stronger than most."

Grayson closed his eyes briefly, relief mixing with the ache of loss. "At least she's alright," he murmured.

Tara leaned forward, her tone firm but gentle. "Grayson, you know as well as I do that Starc and Tomas were soldiers. Like you, they understood the risks of every mission. It doesn't make the loss any easier, but they fought for what they believed in. They wouldn't want you to carry their deaths as a burden."

Grayson looked at her, his eyes heavy with exhaustion and grief. "Doesn't make it hurt less."

"No," Tara agreed softly, "it doesn't. But you'll honor them by continuing to fight for what they believed in. Just like you always have."

She reached over and took a seat beside him, her posture resolute. "And while you recover, I'll be right here. And no," she added, cutting him off before he could protest, "I'm not taking no for an answer."

Grayson gave her a faint, tired smile. "Thank you."

For the first time since waking, the tension in his chest eased slightly. Though the weight of the losses would never truly leave him, knowing Tara was there—steadfast, unyielding—gave him a flicker of strength to face whatever came next.

Amaura sat by the window of her modest room, her gaze drifting over the streets of the capital. It was quiet now, the muffled sounds of life below a soothing contrast to the chaos she had endured. She traced the edge of her teacup with her finger, absently staring into the warm liquid. By all accounts, she was fine. The physicians had said so, even pointing out how the black tendrils that had marked her body after her plunge into the Tether river had vanished completely, except the partial glyph burned into her hand. Her vitals were normal—or as normal as an Aborrent's could be.

And yet, deep inside, something felt... wrong.

Her sister, Tryphena, entered the room, carrying a tray with more tea and some biscuits. "How are you feeling?" she asked, setting the tray down beside Amaura. Her tone was kind, but her eyes carried a hint of caution, as if afraid to push too hard.

"I'm fine," Amaura said, offering a small smile. "At least, that's what the physicians say."

Tryphena sat across from her, folding her hands in her lap. "And what do *you* say?"

Amaura hesitated, her smile faltering. "I don't know. Physically, I feel fine. But inside... it's like there's something lurking. I can't explain it."

"The shock," Tryphena said, nodding knowingly. "That's what they said, right? You went through hell. You need rest."

Amaura looked away, the words not quite comforting. "Maybe."

Tryphena leaned forward, her voice dropping slightly. "You know, I told you so. All of this happened because you trusted Grayson too much."

Amaura stiffened, turning back to her sister. "It's not Grayson's fault," she said firmly. "He didn't know what would happen. And besides, if I hadn't been there, the lich would still be out there, stealing bodies and turning people into undead."

Tryphena sighed, leaning back in her chair. "I know. You're a hero. But tell me, what's the reward for your heroism and self-sacrifice? What do you get for putting your life on the line like that?"

"I don't need a reward," Amaura replied automatically, though her voice carried a hint of defensiveness. "I'm happy to help."

Her sister raised an eyebrow. "That sounds like something you used to say back when we were slaves. Back then, you lived for other people because you didn't have a choice. But you're free now, Amaura. You need to start thinking about yourself for once."

Amaura frowned, her sister's words striking truer than she wanted to admit. "I *do* think about myself," she said softly, though even she didn't sound convinced.

Tryphena didn't push further, simply shaking her head and standing. "I'm just saying, you've earned the right to want something for yourself. Think about it." She turned to leave, pausing at the door. "I'll bring dinner up later."

Amaura watched her go, her chest tightening as her sister's words lingered in her mind. She didn't need a reward—she truly believed that. Helping others was enough. Making a difference was enough.

But still...

Her thoughts drifted to Grayson. She pictured his steady gaze, his quiet determination, and the way he had thrown himself into danger time and again to protect his team—and her. She knew he was grateful, of course. But a small, selfish part of her wished he would say it, that he would acknowledge everything she had done in a way that was just for her. Not as a soldier, or a member of his team, but as *Amaura*.

Amaura unconsciously blushed and briefly smiled for a moment as she pondered to herself, *am I in love?*

She shook her head, brushing the thought aside. She didn't need anything from him. And yet, the faintest trace of hope lingered in her heart, unspoken and fragile.

Grayson leaned against the railing of the hospital grounds, his gaze fixed on the horizon as he took slow, measured breaths. The doctors had insisted on these walks, claiming they were essential for rebuilding his stamina and maintaining his strength. He'd agreed grudgingly, but the truth was, he wanted to be alone—to brood, to process, to grieve.

But Tara had other plans.

"You're late," her voice called, light and teasing.

Grayson turned to see her approaching, a bright contrast to his somber demeanor. She wore a simple outfit—practical and unassuming compared to her royal garb—but there was no dimming her presence. She radiated energy, as if her very insistence on being here was enough to will him to recover.

"I didn't think you'd come today," Grayson said, his tone gruff.

"And leave you to sulk alone?" she quipped. "Not a chance."

He sighed, shaking his head. "You're a princess. You have duties to attend to. You shouldn't be wasting your time walking laps with one of your soldiers."

Tara folded her arms, her expression softening. "This *is* one of my duties. You're part of my guard, and you were injured protecting this kingdom. Ensuring you recover is part of my responsibility. Besides I wanted to tell you I have put together a new research division. The best steam and magi-tek engineers of the kingdom will have your new arm in no time, and other surprises."

Grayson frowned, his instinct to argue warring with the knowledge that he wouldn't win. She always had a way of spinning things in her favor, and he suspected that was part of what made her so effective in her station. "I can walk alone."

"No, you can't," Tara said firmly. "Because I'm not letting you."

Before he could protest further, she started walking, clearly expecting him to follow. Grayson hesitated, then let out a resigned sigh and fell into step beside her.

At first, their walks were confined to the hospital grounds, the quiet paths offering solace but little distraction. Grayson found it difficult to talk, his thoughts inevitably returning to the faces of Starc and Tomas, the friends and soldiers he had failed to protect. But Tara was persistent, her presence a steady, comforting rhythm that he found hard to ignore.

Over time, their walks grew longer. They ventured into the city streets, Tara always staying close to him as they moved through bustling markets and quiet alleys. The sights and sounds of the capital were a welcome distraction, and slowly, Grayson found himself engaging more. When they eventually transitioned to the palace gardens, he realized he no longer dreaded their outings. In fact, he had begun to look forward to them.

They talked about everything and nothing—philosophy, governance, duty, the strange quirks of life in the capital. Grayson was surprised by how much they had in common, their shared ideals forming a foundation for deep conversations. Where they disagreed, Tara proved herself a skilled debater, challenging him to rethink long-held beliefs. More than once, he left their conversations with a new perspective, grudgingly admitting that she might be right.

Her presence became a balm to his wounded soul, her bright energy cutting through the shadows of his grief. Despite himself, he found it hard to remain melancholy when she was around. She had a way of pulling him out of his thoughts, of grounding him in the present moment.

But with that lightness came something else, something Grayson wasn't prepared for. He found himself watching her more closely than he should—taking note of the way her hair caught the sunlight, the way her laughter seemed to warm the air around them. He admired her sharp mind, her wit, her determination, but it went beyond admiration. He was starting to see her in a way that was wholly inappropriate for a member of her guard.

Grayson clenched his jaw, forcing the thoughts down. He owed Tara his loyalty and his respect. She deserved better than a soldier with a broken body and too many ghosts. He wouldn't let himself act on these feelings—he couldn't.

Yet, as they walked side by side through the gardens, Tara's arm brushing his occasionally, it became increasingly difficult to ignore the warmth spreading through his chest. He resolved to push it aside, to focus on his duty. But every step they took together made that vow harder to keep.

Amaura stared at the ceiling of her small bedroom, her hands resting idly on her stomach. She felt like a bird trapped in a gilded cage—safe, yes, but restless, longing for the freedom she'd tasted at the Academy and during her brief time helping Grayson's team. She missed her classes, the challenge of mastering her powers, and the camaraderie of her peers. Most of all, she missed the people who had become so important to her: Tara and Grayson.

Tara had visited a few times to check on her recovery, her presence a brief but welcome reprieve from the monotony. But Amaura could tell the princess was busy, her visits always hurried, her mind clearly preoccupied with other matters. Grayson, meanwhile, was still undergoing his own recovery, and Amaura hadn't mustered the courage to visit him.

She sighed, brushing a strand of her silvery hair from her face. Something inside her still felt wrong. The black tendrils on her skin were gone, but their memory lingered in the form of an unsettling sensation deep within her—a cold, invasive presence that felt as though it were waiting for the right moment to emerge. She had learned to suppress it, to keep it buried beneath her willpower, but the effort left her drained.

Despite her fears, she couldn't ignore the growing ache in her chest. What if Grayson thought she didn't care enough to visit him? What if he believed she was avoiding him?

The final push came from her sister. Tryphena saw her sitting by the window, staring off in the direction of Grayson's hospital once again and daydreaming. She knew her sister's heart well enough to know exactly what she was feeling.

"You should just go to him if you're that worried," Tryphena said, pulling her from her daydream. "I'm sure you're well enough for a small jaunt. Can't be any worse for you than all the nervous pacing you do."

Amaura smiled at her sister. "Yes, you're right. Thank you. I will go right now. If the doctors come by, tell them I didn't go far."

She dressed quickly, choosing a simple but neat outfit. She stepped outside and stopped by a nearby stall to purchase a bouquet of fresh flowers. Their vibrant colors seemed like a small, tangible offering of hope and care. Holding them close, she made her way toward the hospital, her heart pounding with nervous anticipation.

When she arrived, the sight of Grayson walking the hospital grounds brought a smile to her face. His stride was slower than usual, but he was on his feet—a good sign. She quickened her pace, eager to see him, to speak with him.

Then she noticed Tara walking beside him.

Amaura slowed, her steps faltering as she watched them. Tara reached out, her hand brushing against Grayson's before intertwining her fingers with his. The two of them walked side by side, their smiles soft and unguarded, a quiet intimacy passing between them that spoke volumes. They looked like a pair of sweethearts, their connection undeniable.

A pang of jealousy and loneliness struck Amaura like a blow to the chest. She stopped in her tracks, clutching the flowers tightly as her mind raced. She had always admired Tara and cherished their friendship, but in this moment, she couldn't help the sharp edge of envy that rose within her. And Grayson—he had been her hero, her inspiration, the one who had believed in her even when she doubted herself. Seeing them together, so close, felt like a door closing.

The cold presence inside her stirred, feeding on her emotions. For a brief moment, she let it slip free, her control faltering.

The flowers in her hand withered instantly, their vibrant petals curling into brittle husks. Startled, Amaura stared at the bouquet, her breath hitching. Fear and guilt clawed at her chest as she realized what had happened. She had let it out—the thing she had been suppressing, the thing that wasn't supposed to exist. It had twisted something beautiful into something dead.

Panic gripped her. She tossed the withered flowers to the ground, her vision blurring with unshed tears as she turned and fled. She couldn't let them see her like this. She couldn't face Grayson or Tara now—not when she was so unsure of herself, not when she felt like a stranger in her own body.

Amaura retreated toward her home, her heart heavy with shame and sadness. She had wanted to show Grayson that she cared, to remind him that he mattered to her. But now, all she could think about was the cold, dark thing inside her—and the fear that it might one day consume her entirely.

Amaura stumbled through the door of her home, her vision blurred with tears that she could no longer hold back. The moment she saw her sister, Tryphena, standing in the small, familiar space, all her emotions came crashing down like a dam breaking. She burst into sobs, her body trembling as she collapsed into her sister's arms.

Tryphena's expression shifted immediately to one of concern, and she wrapped her arms around Amaura, holding her tightly. "It's alright," she murmured soothingly, stroking Amaura's silvery hair. "Let it out. Whatever it is, we'll face it together."

Amaura clung to her sister, her tears soaking into Tryphena's shoulder. "I... I don't know what's wrong with me," she choked out. "I feel so lost. I can't control it, and—and I'm scared."

"Hush," Tryphena said softly, rocking her gently. "You're strong, Amaura. You've been through worse. Whatever this is, you'll overcome it. You always do."

Amaura nodded weakly, clutching onto her sister like a lifeline. Tryphena was her constant, the one person who had always been there for her, through every hardship, every moment of doubt. She felt safer in her arms, as though the world's weight might not crush her after all.

But as Amaura buried her face in Tryphena's shoulder, she didn't see the subtle shift in her sister's expression. Tryphena's soft, soothing smile turned sharper, colder. A glint of something unspoken—something sinister—flickered in her eyes, and a small glyph glimmered under the band of her bracelet.

Her voice remained gentle, though there was a strange undertone to it now. "It's going to be alright," she whispered. "I'll make sure of it."

Amaura didn't notice. She was too consumed by her pain and fear, too wrapped up in the comfort of her sister's embrace to sense the dark intent lurking beneath the surface.

Epilogue

Jarius sprung up from the dark and bloody altar, screaming as bolts of dark green corrosive energy coursed throughout this body. Even though his "death" was only moments ago, it still felt like eternity. Waking up was just as jarring and painful as he remembered, although he had only gone through the Resurgence once before. As he tried to regain his breath and composure, through the agony, he heard a familiar voice.

"Welcome back, boss." Orzian said as she put away some tools she used to prep the body for the Awakening. Her six-foot-five Oni frame seemed out of place here, but she was always a loyal ally to Jarius. "Didn't go as planned, huh? So, what now? This changes our timeline."

"Hmm…" Jarius evaluated. "Perhaps I need to switch up my strategy. The appearance of this Savant was a glorious surprise, but I don't think the corruption from the Plane of Death will be enough by itself to turn her. The spell's completion was only partial…" He pondered in thought. "Letchen!" Jarius demanded.

A thin and lanky lyrian, with jackal ears and a thin layer of fur over his skin, came into the dark, foreboding room. His shadowy leather suit and stitched cloak only added to his mystique. "You rang?" His bow was an obvious sarcastic gesture.

Jarius, deep in thought, "I have an important mission for you. Hmmm. Yes, yes!" He declared with a creepy smile. "It's not ideal, but this should work." He whispers something to Letchen as if conspiring forces were near. Then, with a casual wave, Jarius dismisses his allies as he casually walks into an adjoining room.

Still pondering, scheming, he effortlessly beckons the Tether to close the door and illuminate the room with dim lighting. He stops before two ancient mirrors, adored with several glyphs and ancient, intricate decorations as though they are artifacts from another century. Jarius performs precise gestures and the glyphs on the mirrors come to life with blazing incandescence the color of the plane of origin to which the spells Tether originates.

The reflective surface of the mirrors becomes fluid and distorted. Jarius waited, still going over his plans in his head, trying to predict the outcomes.

First, the mirror to the left displayed the recipient on its glassy surface. The air pirate, gruff yet handsome face seemed slightly annoyed as he took off his tricorne hat and goggles. "Jarius, I assume you are letting us know this 'strike force' of the princess will no longer be a pain in my side?" Darrian said.

At that moment, the second mirror reveals its patron. Talia, stoic as ever, fills the reflective surface. She wipes a drip of blood away from her lips, which was a stark contrast to her pure, milky white skin. Impatiently, she sighs before addressing her companions, "It's feeding time here in Tanzahar. My tolerance has limits. It's bad enough I lost my best slave over this endeavor. I expect this to be worthwhile!"

"Allies, partners...Friends." The intended barb obvious, Jarius paces, "There have been...interesting developments." Staring at Talia. "Your slave is not only an aborrent but...a 'savant'." Jarius pauses for effect, seemingly very proud of himself. The others did not seem amused.

Talia could hide most of her surprise with only a slight twitch giving her away. Darrian, however, did not disguise his anger, slamming his fist on a nearby desk, then throwing his hands up in the air. "Wait! Are you pulling my tether?" He then stopped in his tracks as though realizing something vitally important. "What about the princess' strike force? They still live? And now they have a savant? Our benefactor will not be pleased."

"Relax. I have the situation in-hand. Her training is inadequate and lacks the self-discipline required. She caught me unprepared. It won't happen again!" Jarius turns. "I have a plan. I will contact you should your participation become necessary."

Jarius has already blocked out their protests as his newly acquired brain calculates the possibilities. He gestures and the lights and mirrors deactivate while he exits the room with a gruesome smile.

About the Author

Charles McGinniss is a lifelong enthusiast of fantasy, science fiction, and storytelling in all its forms. Over two decades ago, he began crafting a richly detailed world for their tabletop RPG group—a world that has since evolved through years of creativity, refinement, and dedication. This immersive setting now serves as the foundation for their latest book, a project that has grown into something deeply personal. More than just a creative endeavor, this work represents the author's enduring love for imaginative fiction and the boundless potential of storytelling. Hoping the world, they've created will continue to grow and inspire others long beyond their own journey, Charles McGinniss invites readers to step into a universe crafted with care, heart, and vision.

Acknowledgements

I have to start by thanking my amazing wife, Trecia. She has been a solid supporter and my number one fan. This could not have been possible without her patience, love, and understanding. Her input, suggestions, and proofreading were a monumental help. You have always had my back and I am so lucky to have you in my life. I love you.

This work also owes a great deal to the love and support of my mother, Rita. I appreciate and can never repay all you have done for me in my life.

Also, a shout out to my friends and co-gamers who have put up with me all these years; Mike, Bill, Dave, Pat and many more.

Finally, in remembrance of our friend lost much too soon. Rob, you were the most incredible person, and you are missed every day.